A Question of Courage

IRENE MORCK

Western Producer Prairie Books
Saskatoon, Saskatchewan

Western Producer Prairie Books
Saskatoon, Saskatchewan

Cover illustration by Oni
Cover design by Warren Clark/GDL
Edited by Diana J. Wieler

Printed and bound in Canada

The publisher acknowledges the support received for this publication from the Canada Council.

Western Producer Prairie Books is a unique publishing venture located in the middle of western Canada and owned by a group of prairie farmers who are members of Saskatchewan Wheat Pool. From the first book in 1954, a reprint of a serial originally carried in the weekly newspaper *The Western Producer,* to the book before you now, the tradition of providing enjoyable and informative reading for all Canadians is continued.

Canadian Cataloguing in Publication Data

Morck, Irene, 1944–

A question of courage

ISBN 0-88833-257-2

I. Title.

PS8576.063Q4 1988 jC813′.54 C88-098087-7
PZ7.M77Qu 1988

To my sister, Ruthie Casey, who insisted that I write this book
To my husband, Mogens Nielsen, who made it possible
And to my mom, Marion Morck, who never quit praying

Chapter 1

"Gee! Was that fun!" shouted my little sister Colleen, pulling tightly on her horse's reins as he pranced in circles. "Keri, you've got to try it. Feels weird at first, but it's so exciting."

I looked down past Fancy's shiny brown shoulders, down to the far-away ground, gulped, and remained motionless.

"Not a fast gallop, Keri. Just a nice slow canter. You'll like it once you get going. Honest, you will."

I took a deep breath, loosened my reins, and gently squeezed Fancy's sides.

From a standstill, my horse lifted her long legs into a canter. The power of it slammed me against the back of the saddle, then slid me sideways. My right hand grabbed the saddle horn, my left yanked the reins frantically. Fancy jerked to a stop, throwing me completely off balance, and the ground rushed up to meet me.

I lay on the dusty grass, my right knee and shoulder aching.

"Keri, Keri!" Colleen sounded frantic.

I forced my eyes to open, and looked away through hot tears. "Don't tell Mom and Dad. Please."

She helped pull me up. "Can you walk?"

I took a few painful steps.

"Colleen, I mean it. Don't tell Mom or Dad."

"Why not? You didn't do anything wrong. They'll have to know why you're limping."

"Please."

"OK, it's up to you. What do you want to do now?"

She was hoping I'd want to try again. Instead, I mumbled, "Let's take the horses back home. My knee and shoulder are really sore."

That night, my head swirled with fitful dreams of falling, of landing, of aching all over. The next morning I groaned when I moved out of bed and put weight on my sore knee. I did my best not to limp while I was setting the breakfast table. Mom watched me carefully as I walked back and forth between the cupboards and the table, and I was surprised that she didn't question me.

When Dad came in for breakfast, he said, "Wanda's got foot rot." I moaned. Wanda was the most enormous cow we'd ever owned, and definitely the meanest. I called her Wicked Wanda the Witch.

Dad ignored my moan. "Luckily I noticed Wanda limping when she came home with some of the other cows for water this morning. I closed the gate before they could get out."

He poured milk on his porridge. "We'll probably be able to bale hay right after lunch because there wasn't much dew last night, so we'd better get out right away and give Wanda some penicillin."

The idea of running after any cow with my sore leg was bad enough, but Wanda! Why did it have to be her? Wanda chased me whenever she got a chance. She seemed to respect everybody else. I always begged Mom and Dad to sell Wanda, but every year she produced the biggest calf in our herd. Our cows were not for milking; we fattened calves for market, so any cow that raised a big calf was doing her job.

Dad always said, "All you have to do is stay away from Wanda a week or two after she's got her new calf every spring. That's the only time she's really mean. The rest of the year you just gotta call her bluff."

Out we went to the corral with penicillin, syringe, and needle to treat Wanda for her infected foot.

The cows were milling around the corral, bawling indignantly while the calves tried to follow their mothers and snatch breakfast on the run.

Dad, Mom, and Colleen carried light whips, but I grabbed a big stick as protection. It was terrifying to be in the midst of huge cows pushing and shoving around in a small space. It wasn't going to be easy to cut Wanda away from the rest of the herd, and to chase her into the squeeze for her injection was going to be very difficult indeed.

As we approached Wanda, she lunged away, yanking the nipple out of her calf's mouth. The little guy's tongue stayed out, curved in the sucking position, with a string of milk slobber hanging from his foam-covered lips, and wide puzzled eyes that seemed to say, "Hey, what happened?" I would have laughed if I hadn't been so scared.

We chased Wanda, although as usual I hung back and let the others do most of the crowding. Bellowing, Wanda swerved and twisted and lurched. An old range cow knows that whatever people want to do to her is probably not going to feel too pleasant, so she gets wily and frantic. Wanda was just one old cow with a sore, swollen foot, and there were four of us, but we were puffing by the time we finally got her into the small holding corral. Her calf bawled, and scrambled in beside her.

My knee was throbbing. We still had to chase Wanda into the squeeze, a high narrow alley made of thick wooden planks. In a squeeze, a cow can't move around while she's getting injected. Wanda knew from experience that painful things happened in the squeeze, and she had no intention of going in.

Cracking their whips and shouting, Dad, Mom, and Colleen managed to chase her several times right up to the squeeze, but each time Wanda spun and darted between them, back to the other side of the pen.

"Keri, come on," Dad yelled. "Do some good! Move right in. Crowd her so she can't get past. Come on!"

There was no use arguing. Terrified, I limped along close to Colleen as she swung her whip and yelled to head Wanda toward the squeeze again. The stick vibrated in my trembling hand. Wanda was almost at the squeeze when she looked sideways, spun around, and roared straight for me, her head down.

"Wave your stick," Dad shouted. I stood petrified as Wanda charged, her massive head lowered, closer, closer . . .

"Swing your stick. Yell at her!" Mom screamed.

Wanda was almost at me when Colleen reached her, hollering, slashing her whip around Wanda's face. That huge cow bellowed and swung away.

I stood shaking.

"You've got to show her you're not scared," shouted Dad.

"But I *am* scared."

"Well, you can't let her know. Please, Keri, you are fifteen years old." He gulped, and looked around. "We need everybody to be useful on this farm . . ."

"Yeah, like Colleen." I was trembling. "I hate Colleen. I hate all of you!" I shrieked, and ran into the house.

No one came running after me.

The ache in my knee was mild compared to the ache in my chest. I lay on my bed staring at fly specks on the ceiling and light fixture, listening to the bawling of cows and calves. Then after a while I heard the joyous mooing of cattle free again. So, they had managed to chase Wanda into the squeeze, inject her, and then let the cows out to pasture.

Nothing was mentioned about my outburst. Quiet and strained, we ate an early lunch. At haying time, Mom always drove the tractor that pulled the baler, and Dad ran the bale wagon to pick up the bales and stack them.

As she climbed into the tractor, Mom smiled awkwardly at us. "I'm afraid that you girls have to do some weeding in the garden this afternoon." Above all things, Colleen hated weeding. She didn't talk to me all afternoon, and it seemed strange not to hear her complaints.

While we weeded, hardly making a dent in the huge garden, I kept remembering Wanda's beady eyes and lowered head coming at me. And I thought of my fall off Fancy. How on earth was I going to get the nerve to try cantering again?

That evening when it came time to collect the eggs, Colleen muttered, "I don't see why you can't collect eggs. It's not fair that I always have to do it."

Alone I walked into the darkness of the chicken coop, nauseated by the thick musty smell, stepping to avoid as much fresh chicken poop as possible.

The hens guarding their nests cackled in warning, sensing my terror. I reached furtively under the crisp feathered breasts to steal their day's labour, and most of them pecked with their sharp beaks at my hand. One big hen pecked so hard that I yanked my hand away empty, and had to try again and again, each time receiving another peck before I finally became desperate enough to grab her egg.

Colleen never had trouble gathering eggs. The hens might cluck their disapproval, but they never pecked at her.

Supper was as quiet as lunch had been. I was wishing it was over so that I could go hide in my room, when the phone rang. Mom got up to answer it. "Susan!" she squeaked joyously, "How are you?"

We knew better than to even clatter a dish when Susan Spalding phoned from Toronto. Susan had always been Mom's best friend, all the way back to grade one when they were little neighbour kids in Calgary.

"Susan, that's wonderful!" I had never heard Mom so thrilled.

We all stopped chewing to listen. "Oh, and you won't believe this. There are two acreages for sale right around here. It wouldn't be much of a drive for Ben. Only about forty minutes. You know poor old Mrs. Martin died this spring. I guess I wrote you about that. So there's her place. And the Kraulis place is for sale. Yeah, two miles north. It's a big modern house. But Mrs. Martin's place is nice too, and we'd be closer."

Mom was so excited she was trembling. "And Diane can go on the school bus with Keri. Rosewood isn't going to be teaching higher than grade six any more. So starting this September, they're bussing junior and senior high kids into the big school in Moreland." Mom paused for breath. "How soon would you be coming? I can't believe it. Oh, it's so wonderful!"

When Mom got off the phone, her words scrambled with excitement. "They're moving back. Ben's just got word. He's being transferred back to Calgary. The manager there just quit. And they're tired of living in big cities, so they've decided to buy an acreage. Maybe they'll even buy one of these around here. Maybe even Mrs. Martin's place. Oh, I'm so happy!"

"When are they coming?" we all asked, excited too.

"They're flying out here next Thursday to look at acreages. Then they'll go back and pack all their stuff so they can get settled before school starts. Oh, isn't it wonderful?

"And do we ever have lots to do before they get here!" Mom's eyes were dancing. "Let's see, this is Friday. The house needs a real cleaning, the lawn needs cutting, the garden needs weeding . . ."

"Hold on, Elaine." Dad grinned. "You and I have to get some hay baled before they get here."

It isn't hard to figure out what Colleen and I did that week. Colleen talked me into leaving the weeding until last, insisting that the Spaldings would first notice an uncut lawn and a messy house.

Diane was coming. We'd had lots of fun together as little

kids, except that maybe she had always been a bit too wild for me; Diane would try anything. But five years is a long time. What would she be like now? Would she even want to be my friend?

It was as though Colleen read my thoughts. One evening, while we were feeding the chickens, she asked, "Do you think Diane will have changed very much?"

"Probably. I guess we've changed. So she must have too. Hey, Col . . ."

"What?"

I finally blurted out what I'd been trying to make myself say for days. "Thanks for rescuing me from Wanda, and I'm sorry about what I said . . ."

"Ah, it's OK." Her eyes looked wet, and she laughed with a funny little catch in her voice. "I'll collect the eggs tonight."

The next morning Dad looked around the kitchen. "Boy, this sure is a shiny floor. And the yard never looked so good. You girls have been doing a lot of work this week. You can take a little time off, you know, if you want to go riding or something. I'm sure the Spaldings don't expect this farm to look picture perfect. Even slaves get a few hours off once in a while." He grinned at Mom. "If it's OK with the slavedriver, of course."

Mom made a face at him, but she laughed. "Well, maybe you could try to get some more of the garden weeded this morning, and then ride this afternoon."

While we hacked at the weeds, I thought of Diane. If *she* had a horse, she'd be able to ride it. Trot, gallop, everything. I knew she would, and she'd think I should be able to do those things too. That's just the way she was.

Two more days until she arrived. I could do it. I had to do it. Colleen had said it felt great once you got going. Kneeling there in the dirt of our garden, it was easy to imagine myself flying over the fields on Fancy, soaring in that magical rocking-chair motion. My knee and shoulder felt as good as new, and the sun burned the sky a deep rich blue. Today would be as good a time as ever.

"Keri, do you feel like riding this afternoon?" asked Colleen, leaning on her hoe, just before we went in for lunch.

"You bet!"

Mom was driving the baler out of the yard as we rode off. She looked at me and said gently, "Be careful."

So she did know that I'd fallen.

Colleen and I rode down the lane. The only noise was the rhythmic thud of hooves on dirt. Peaceful, that was the word for it. Yet inside I felt tight, like a stretched rubber band.

Chapter 2

We turned west, and rode past Mrs. Martin's old house. I had loved the old lady with her beautiful flower arrangements, her delicious pastries, her friendly curiosity. "How come Mrs. Martin had to die?" Colleen said, her voice slow and sad. "I sure miss her." Then she looked up at me. "Keri, do you think Spaldings will buy her acreage?"

"Probably."

"Do you hope they do?"

"I don't know. Sure, I guess I do."

We rode another kilometre or so. Colleen pointed out a wild flower, a beautiful shadow pattern of trees against a fence, a little mouse that scampered through the grass in front of Fancy's feet. I began to realize that she wasn't going to bring up the subject of cantering.

I should have been grateful for her understanding, but somehow, I felt more tense. My optimism from that morning had melted.

"I should try again today." My tight dry throat made the sound come out like a whisper.

"Aw, Keri, why not wait for another time? Today we can just walk the horses. It's too nice a day to hurry."

I shook my head, fighting the small surge of panic under my ribs. It couldn't wait. All I had was two days.

I looked up to find Colleen staring at me, her head tilted.

"It's her, isn't it?" she said quietly. "Diane. It's because she's coming."

I nodded, relieved that I didn't have to say the words myself. Colleen was just a kid, but she could be so smart sometimes.

"When do you want to try?" she asked.

I took a deep breath. "Right now. The horses won't run as fast headed away from home."

"I've got a good idea. Let's go back home so you can try your first galloping down our lane, headed away from the house. They sure won't run fast then."

Sensing her excitement, Pony Bill started prancing. I was always glad Fancy didn't prance like Pony Bill. He was such a spunky little horse, full of life, kinda like a sports car. Colleen and Pony Bill made a good pair.

It didn't take long to get home, with Pony Bill prancing and Fancy trotting. "At least a gallop should be smoother than a trot," I said to Colleen.

"Sure is." She laughed. "And smoother than a prance too."

When we reached our yard, Colleen turned Pony Bill back toward the road, loosened his reins, and away they went, Pony Bill cantering, Colleen bouncing. At the end of the lane, they turned and galloped back. By the time she reached me, Colleen was balancing quite well considering it was only her second time galloping. Her face glowed, and she puffed as though she had been running. "Is that ever great! It's hard to balance at first, but you get used to it. Wow!"

My heart was pounding so loudly I wondered if Fancy could sense it. I looked at the ground. Gee, Fancy was tall.

Why couldn't she have been smaller, like Pony Bill? But she was gentle. And everybody always said that she was just the right size for me because I'm so tall. Why did I have to be such a chicken?

Here goes nothing, I thought.

The minute Fancy broke into a canter, I felt myself slipping, and yanked on her reins. Poor Fancy slid to a stop, with me perched precariously to one side of the saddle.

I had to try again.

This time we didn't even get one step before my tense body slipped, and I pulled us to a stop. I was trembling by now, frustrated, humiliated, and terrified. Fancy was quivering too, her sensitive mouth not used to such jerking on the bit. She wanted to please, but was totally confused.

I could hardly hold back the tears.

"Why don't we try another day?" said Colleen.

"No. I've got to do it now." I clenched my teeth, staring at that far-away hard ground.

"Try knotting your reins so they can hang loose over the horn. Then hold on with both hands so you're not tempted to yank back on the reins."

That sounded like good advice. This time I started out gripping the horn, my knuckles white, but those stupid hands still flew up to grab the reins and jerk her to a stop. It was terrible, being out of control, moving with such power.

"Don't touch the reins."

"But it feels like she might run away."

"Naw, she's not going to run away. Just let her go and hang on," Colleen shouted. "Try again!"

"Easy for you to say," I yelled, angry now. This time, I hung on for a few steps before my hands automatically grabbed the reins and slid Fancy to the same jolting stop. And then it happened again. Down I went, landing this time in a willow bush at the side of the lane.

I can't stand it, I thought, lying spread like an old rag doll on the bush with Fancy sniffing my back end, and Colleen trying unsuccessfully not to laugh.

"Go away," I shouted. "I wish you weren't my sister." Colleen's lip quivered and she turned to ride slowly toward the yard.

"Col! Please! Come back. I didn't mean that."

She dragged me from the willow bush, and gently brushed me off. We both knew I wasn't hurt physically, but still it felt good to cry together under the hot July sun. Without speaking, we led our horses home.

While we unsaddled the horses, Matilda kept rubbing against my legs and purring. I picked up my fluffy grey cat and held her tight. When we went into the house, I winced as always to have to shut the door in Matilda's face. Mom never allowed a cat in the house. Strange how Colleen and I could love cats so much and have a mom who hated them.

I went up to my bedroom and lay on the bed, staring at my horse pictures on the wall, wishing that Matilda could be purring and snuggling beside me. After a few minutes I went back out to the barn, and sat on a straw bale, holding her on my lap. The Spaldings were to arrive in less than forty-eight hours.

The barn door opened, and in came Colleen. "Hi," she said, "I thought you might be here."

We stayed in the barn until it was time to make supper. Mom and Dad always expected us to have supper ready when they came home from the field.

The next day we didn't have time to ride, and after supper I watched with jealousy as Mom, exhausted from eight hours of baling hay, stayed up late to bake an angel food cake. One thing that Diane's mom and I have in common is our passion for angel food cake, but Mom had never ever baked one for me, not even for my birthday. She always said, "They're too much nuisance to make, and then what do you do with all the yolks?"

I hardly recognized Diane when I saw her at the airport. She was almost as tall as me, and just as thin, but there the resemblance ended. She looked beautiful. Her hair shone gold, her blue eyes were ringed expertly with make-up, her nails were painted pale pink the same colour as her lipstick. She walked confidently beside her parents, smiling regally as they strode towards us. I tried to smooth my dark, mousy, fly-away hair, and smiled uneasily, my stomach tight.

On the way back from the airport, sandwiched in the back seat beside Mr. Spalding, Colleen, Diane, and I chatted about old memories, just as our mothers were doing in the front seat beside Dad. We talked about adventures we'd had together over the years, but even on that ride home, Diane didn't waste any time letting Colleen and I know that living in Toronto was nothing like living on a farm.

Before supper Colleen and I had to feed the two orphan calves and the chickens. Diane followed us around, rambling on about colours of lipstick, the latest in fashions, the exciting guys at school in Toronto, her handsome ski instructor, . . .

The chickens came squawking for their food, mobbing us as usual, and Diane said, "Do you remember Devil the rooster?"

I winced. "Yeah."

"I'll never forget how he used to chase you, Keri, and peck your ankles until they bled. And Colleen, you were so little, but such a terror! You used to yell at Devil and chase him away from Keri, do you remember?"

"No." Colleen looked at the ground.

"I guess you'd have been too young to remember. You were still in diapers then, so you were probably less than two. We must have been about six."

Neither Colleen nor I answered, but Diane kept on. "Funny how Devil never chased me or anybody else. Remember, your dad always begged you to stand up to Devil, but he finally had to chop off Devil's head and get a smarter rooster."

"Smarter?" asked Colleen.

"Sure." Diane laughed. "Smart enough not to get his head cut off."

"I'll see you guys," Colleen said. "I'm going to gather the eggs."

Diane was fascinated by our horses. "They're gorgeous. When did you get them?"

"About three months ago."

"How come you call this one *Pony* Bill? He's way too big to be a pony."

"I guess because Fancy is so much taller. Dad started calling him that, and the name just stuck."

"A couple of the richest girls in my class in Toronto had horses and did dressage and entered in horse shows. Mom and Dad said I can have a horse when we get settled out here." When we left the pasture, she paused and turned around for one more look.

The next morning Diane appeared at the breakfast table with freshly painted orange-red fingernails that matched her lipstick, and declared, "I'd like to ride a horse this morning." She laughed. "Do you think the horse will know these are designer jeans, not riding jeans?"

Colleen wrinkled her face. Diane's mom smiled. "Keri and Colleen, do you think Diane could try riding one of your horses?"

Mom answered. "Of course she can. I'm sure the girls would be glad to show her how."

"But, Mom, I have to finish weeding the garden," said Colleen. Then I knew how badly she wanted out of this. Mom looked to me with pleading eyes.

"Sure, I'll help Diane." It would be more fun than weeding the garden. "Which do you want to try, Fancy or Pony Bill?"

"Doesn't matter to me." She smiled, waving those orange-red fingernails.

After breakfast we fitted Diane with Mom's cowboy boots. Before Dad left to cultivate the summerfallow, he came out to the barn where I was saddling the horses. "Let Diane start with Fancy. Pony Bill might be too much for her at first." He ruffled my hair and grinned. "Good luck with your riding lessons, Miss Andersen."

I led Fancy to the house. Diane sauntered out, her hands in her pockets, letting me know this was no big deal.

"OK," I said, "you get on a horse from the left side. Put your left foot in the stirrup, grab the saddle horn, give a hop, and up you go." She was slow and awkward in pulling herself up, and the saddle slipped down, crooked.

I loosened the cinch and straightened the saddle again on Fancy's back. "Just a minute, Diane, I'll get a box for you to stand on. Otherwise the saddle might pull over again. Fancy's so tall to get up on."

Diane sighed, and looked bored.

Rushing to bring back the old wooden box from beside the gas tank, I tripped and fell, sprawling on the gravel. My scrapes stung, but they were nothing compared to Diane's comment, "You're kinda clumsy today, aren't you?" She giggled. "Just joking." I began to envy Colleen weeding the garden.

I led Fancy around the yard while Diane got used to the motion of a horse walking. At first she clutched the horn, but soon she relaxed and smiled. I started to relax too.

Within a few minutes, Diane was ready to try steering by herself, and was delighted to find that Fancy would indeed obey her, turning, stopping, backing up.

"It's fun!" she said, grinning, and I felt better.

"How do you make her run?" Diane asked a couple of minutes later.

A knot gripped my stomach. "Do you mean trot?"

"Whatever."

"Are you sure you're ready to try trotting? It's rough and fast and a lot different from walking."

"Just tell me how, and let me decide for myself."

"Hold the reins in and gently squeeze both her sides with your legs."

As Fancy started to trot, Diane grabbed the horn with one

hand, yanking the reins with the other. Fancy slid to a stop, with Diane slipping to one side of the saddle.

"Maybe that's enough for today," I said, but Diane surprised me. "No way. I'm going to do it."

And she did. Bouncing and jiggling and sliding, she didn't look too impressive, but she did manage to stay on. After a few more times trotting around the yard, she declared, "This is great!"

"If you want, we can go for a little ride together now. But we'll just walk the horses."

"Why? I'm not scared of running."

"You're just learning, and you shouldn't rush things."

"You're scared."

My face flushed. "Why should I be scared? Of what?"

"I don't know. That's just you. Let's go." Diane turned Fancy and headed for the barn where Pony Bill was standing tied and saddled.

"Would you like to try Pony Bill?" I asked, hoping, praying that she would say yes. Maybe his liveliness would bring her down a peg or two.

"Naw. I'll stick with Fancy. She's so tall and elegant."

"Pony Bill's kinda prancy. So maybe it's best that I ride him."

"Oh. Well, maybe I *should* try him."

Surprised but relieved, I adjusted the stirrups on his saddle for Diane while she surveyed her fingernails one by one. "Your horses sure are dirty, aren't they? Just look at my hands! My friends' horses in Toronto weren't dirty like this."

"That's because our horses don't live in a stable. They're always out in the pasture, and they have a favourite old dirt hole that they love to roll in."

"Couldn't you wash them before you go riding?"

"We wouldn't have time to wash them every time we want to go for a ride."

Hardly talking, we walked the horses almost a kilometre through the soft dirt that Dad had just cultivated. He waved to us from the tractor and turned the blinker lights on to say hi, something that usually delighted me. It didn't make me feel much better that day.

A wind had blown up, a cold wind that made goose pimples rise on my bare arms. Pony Bill was starting to prance. "Boy, he's exciting to ride," said Diane.

"Maybe we should soon be getting back. It's almost lunch time."

"Yeah, it's getting kinda cold too."

We turned the horses and headed home. "Which horse is faster, Fancy or Pony Bill?" asked Diane.

"Fancy, by far."

"How do you know? Have you ever raced them flat out?" I felt she was trying to trap me, to make me admit I couldn't ride a galloping horse.

"You can ask Mom or Dad or Colleen. We've all watched Fancy and Pony Bill race across the fields lots of times, like when a storm is brewing or if you whistle for them to come and get oats. Fancy can always outrun Pony Bill with no trouble at all."

"Prove it," Diane shouted. "Race you back!"

My heart froze.

She kicked Pony Bill. That was the wrong thing to do. He took off at a full gallop towards home. Diane screamed and clutched the horn with both hands. The knotted reins flapped against his neck and he galloped faster. "Help! Keri! Help!"

"Pull on the reins," I yelled. But she just continued screaming and kept both hands glued to the horn. "Pull the reins," I shouted again.

Shouting was useless. I would have to catch up and grab the reins to stop him. Colleen would have done it.

Fancy was getting excited, seeing Pony Bill race home. I held her to a bone-jolting trot, fighting her anxiousness. You can do it, I said to myself. You've got to do it.

Diane was slipping badly.

All I had to do was gallop alongside and grab those reins. It wouldn't be so bad.

I loosened my reins a bit. Fancy broke into a gallop. That frightening blur of power and speed hit me full in the face. I yanked her to a stop; I couldn't help it.

And I watched, sick to my stomach, as Diane fell, and lay crumpled in the dirt, silent and motionless.

Chapter 3

Dad had seen it all. He came running across the field, shouting, "Why didn't you catch up to her and stop Pony Bill? You didn't even try!"

When he reached Diane, he bent over, trembling, and touched her shoulder. "Diane! Are you OK? Talk to me. Diane!"

She was white, oh so white. And she had fallen head first. I was shaking, the sharp knot in my chest threatening to cut off my breath completely.

Dad scooped Diane up and ran for home, holding her close, tripping over rocks in his hurry, completely ignoring me. Despite the wind, I could hear the tractor running and Fancy's soft breathing as I led her, following Dad.

I never thought I'd be happy to hear someone moan. But there it was, a soft, wrung-out sound coming from the limp bundle in Dad's arms. Relief rose in my chest like a bird struggling to fly.

She moaned again, and Dad's taut face lit up too. He

stopped for a minute. "Diane?" Her eyes flickered, she groaned, and looked up at his face. Then she started to howl.

Dad shifted her weight and kept running. The others rushed out to meet us.

"What happened?" our mothers shrieked together, drowning out Diane's howling.

Dad had to shout too. "Pony Bill ran away with Diane."

"Why didn't you stop him, Keri?" Mom cried. "Fancy could easily catch up to him!"

"'Cause she's a wimp!" screamed Diane. It was the first thing she'd said since her fall, and I knew then that she was going to be all right. But those words stung so deeply that I shuddered.

Everybody turned to me as Diane spat out the next words. "I could have been killed. And she didn't do a thing to stop him." She started to cry again, louder than before.

"But I told you not to run him," I sobbed.

Colleen followed me silently into the house, and sat beside me on my bed. Our car started and zoomed off. They would be taking Diane to Moreland to get her checked at the hospital.

I looked down at my new pink bedspread. "I'd run away, Col, but I don't know where I would go."

"Oh, Keri." She disappeared. I heard the screen door slam. A few minutes later, it slammed again. Colleen climbed the squeaky wooden stairs and padded into my bedroom. And there in her arms was Matilda. I buried my face in the soft warm fur and cried silently.

About four hours later, they returned from the hospital. The doctor had x-rayed and examined Diane carefully. There seemed to be nothing wrong. But because she had been knocked out by the fall, Diane was to take it easy over the next few days.

While we were eating supper, I sat quietly as the others made a fuss over Diane. I wished I dared to voice my churning thoughts. So what if I never ever learned to canter? What if I never even got on a horse again? The world wouldn't stop turning. In thirty years, who would even care about what happened today? Nobody but me. Somehow, it had become so important to me. But why?

I pulled my mind back to reality to hear Dad's comment, ". . . better that you fell off Pony Bill instead of Fancy. So much less distance to fall." Everyone agreed.

That started my wheels turning. What if I had a much shorter horse? As short as Pony Bill or even smaller. But definitely not prancy. Short and gentle. Then I wouldn't be so afraid. If only I could find the right horse, and then persuade Mom and Dad to buy it . . .

The conversation gradually drifted to the Spalding's impending move. I scarcely paid any attention from then on, thinking about the new little horse I would find. Somehow, somewhere, there had to be just the right one.

But what reason could I give my parents for wanting another horse, without admitting that I was too much of a chicken to gallop on our own horses? They would have to know, otherwise I could never get anywhere with my plans.

My chance came the next morning. I woke up very early. In the silent house I mixed milk replacer formula, then strolled to the barn to feed Ernie and Patches. Orphan calves appreciate everything you do for them. They wiggle their tails, bunt their heads in the milk pail, scatter milk and foam all over your clothes, but still, they make you feel important and loved.

I heard a noise and thought it must be Matilda hunting a mouse.

"Hi, Skalawag."

I looked up, shocked.

"Dad, what are you doing up so early?"

"I could ask the same thing. It's only six o'clock."

I did my best to pull my face into a smile. "Couldn't sleep."

He sat on the straw bale beside me. "Something's wrong isn't it?"

I couldn't meet his eyes. "What do you mean?"

"Why didn't you catch up to Pony Bill and stop him? Were you mad at Diane? Did you two have a fight? But even that wouldn't make sense. It just isn't like you to want anybody to get hurt. Why . . . ?"

I turned away, but forced myself to answer. "I can't canter."

"Of course you can. You girls run those horses all over the place. What do you mean you can't canter?"

I looked up at the dirty rafters, and spoke through clenched teeth. "I can't canter. I can trot. But any time I try cantering, I just fall off or pull Fancy to a stop."

Dad touched my shoulder. "Why haven't you told us before?"

"Because you already think I'm coward enough. I know you do. I hate it when you're ashamed of me. Diane's right. I'm an absolute wimp."

"Everything takes practice, Skalawag."

My eyes flooded with tears. "Not for Colleen. She could gallop the first time she tried."

He put his arm around me, and just at that moment Matilda happened to rub against my leg. I couldn't help laughing. Dad gave me a Kleenex to blow my nose and wipe my eyes.

Then I told him of all my attempts and failures at cantering, and it felt so good to talk to him. Finally, I gathered a deep breath and said, "Dad, if only I had a little horse, gentle like Fancy, but really little, maybe I wouldn't be so scared. You even said last night that it was good that Diane fell off Pony Bill instead of Fancy because she didn't have so far to fall."

He shook his head. "No, Keri, that's not the way you need to do things. Getting a smaller horse isn't going to help. Fancy's the right size for you, and she's as gentle as they come." His voice seemed to harden. "You can learn to canter on her. I know you can."

I looked away and fought to keep the tears from starting again.

"Let's go make breakfast," Dad said. "We'll talk about this later."

"How are you?" I asked timidly when Diane came down for breakfast. She turned her head and looked away. Her mother took me aside. "Keri, don't mind Diane, she's stiff and sore this morning. Doesn't feel much like talking to anybody."

Right after breakfast, Mom took the Spaldings to see the two acreages for sale.

They returned for lunch, beaming, to say that they had chosen the Kraulis acreage because it had more room, including a study for Ben and a huge bedroom for Diane. "But we'll still be only two miles away," said Mrs. Spalding.

"Within easy riding distance," Mom added. "You girls can ride back and forth all the time." Diane groaned.

Mrs. Spalding fidgeted with her spoon. "I'm sure it'll be wonderful."

The Spaldings returned to Toronto the next day, and our life slid back to normal. Mom and Dad were busy haying again, and Colleen and I finally had a chance to talk. I told her about my idea of getting a shorter horse.

"Might work." She looked thoughtful.

"Dad sure doesn't think so. I talked to him about it and got nowhere."

"I guess there's no extra money around to buy another horse," said Colleen.

"Hey, Col, I've just thought of a better idea. Maybe I could borrow Mr. Hanson's little white pony for a while. He's always talking about how gentle his sweet Sandy is, and she sure is small enough."

"That might be good. At least it wouldn't cost anything."

Mom and Dad came home early one afternoon, thrilled to announce that they were finally all finished haying. I thought this would be a good time to bring up my idea of borrowing Mr. Hanson's pony instead of buying a new little horse. I begged and pleaded, but got nowhere with that idea either.

And then one evening I heard something. Colleen and I were making supper in the kitchen and through the open window I could hear Mom and Dad talking as they walked through the yard. Their voices were soft but I caught enough of their conversation to realize it was a serious subject: me and my riding. A few steps from the house, Mom said, "Maybe best to wait 'til she's settled in school." Colleen and I looked at each other and I knew she'd heard too. Then the door opened and Mom and Dad were inside, smiling normally. That was the last I heard about horses or riding, for a while.

The Spaldings were back on the evening of August 23, and the comfortable peace ended. Shoving furniture, unpacking boxes, arranging cupboards . . . Well, it wasn't exactly my idea of fun, but it felt good to be doing something for Diane's parents. They were acting so friendly to me, probably because Diane wasn't.

That week we were incredibly busy helping the Spaldings settle in, but we weren't allowed to miss any news – in our community you never could. Not with Mrs. Abigail Trunbowl around. We were still in bed one morning when the phone rang. I heard Mom run to answer it. "Oh, good morning, Mrs. Trunbowl," Mom said groggily. "How are you?"

As I set the breakfast table, I eavesdropped, wondering what earth-shattering news had made Mrs. Trunbowl rise so early. Mom managed to hang up before her porridge got too cold, and she was smirking.

"Guess what, Keri," Mom said in her best teasing voice, "some new people have just bought Mrs. Martin's acreage. And of course Mrs. Trunbowl has already visited them to check them out, and she knows you'll be just thrilled to hear that they have a handsome son the same age as you."

I rolled my eyes. "Oh, thank you, Mrs. Trunbowl!" Colleen giggled, and Mom and Dad joined in the laughter.

Two new sets of neighbours within a few days. I guess everybody wanted to do their moving before school started, so they didn't have to uproot their kids in the middle of the school year.

I sure wasn't looking forward to starting school next week. It would feel strange to be on a different bus from Colleen for the first time, and worse to go to such a big school. After our little Rosewood country school with two grades in most classrooms, it was frightening to imagine Moreland School, with five or six classes of each grade. And they'd be mostly city kids, because Moreland was a "bedroom community" of Calgary, meaning that thousands of people had moved out to Moreland and surrounding acreages, but still commuted to Calgary for work. Their kids would be attending my new school.

That first day came too soon. But as I climbed alone onto the school bus, it thrilled me as always to see that Jennifer Cowie had saved me a seat. Such a gorgeous, popular girl, and yet she acted so friendly to me. Of course I figured she probably wouldn't like me if she really got to know me, so I was always careful to do and say things I thought she'd approve of. We didn't see each other outside of school, but Jennifer was as close as I'd ever come to having a best friend.

That morning we chatted a little, then I stared out the window, knowing that the bus would soon be arriving at Diane's place.

"Hey, Keri, what are you thinking about?" Jennifer asked.

"Oh, the new school, and everything. I hope we can be in the same class."

"Me too." Jennifer smiled. "Did you see that new guy from Mrs. Martin's place?" she whispered, motioning towards the back of the bus. "He's really something."

I turned casually, glancing around as though I were just looking at everyone.

"Good-looking, eh?" said Jennifer. "But he's kinda shy, I think. I wonder if he'll be in our class." I could see the Spaldings' house now.

"I've heard they might have put all the kids from our bus together in the same class, but I'm not sure," said Jennifer.

When the bus stopped, somebody shouted, "Hey, another new kid!"

"Oh wow, that's no *kid,*" said Ron Vander, whistling through his teeth. Everybody watched Diane make her entrance. She was wearing a flamingo-pink shirt, with matching pink earrings, nail polish, and lipstick. Thick blue eye-shadow and heavy black mascara made her eyes look enormous.

Personally, I thought she looked crazy, but it was obvious that the boys were impressed, and even Jennifer said hi in a tone of voice that she never used with me. "Diane," I said, "meet my friends, Jennifer Cowie, Linda Evans . . ."

"Me too," shouted Ron, imitating a panting dog. "Introduce me too." Everybody laughed, even the bus driver.

As the bus drove into Moreland, past luxurious houses twice the size of ours, the knife turned more sharply in my stomach. By the time we arrived at the huge Moreland School, I was ready to walk back home.

The hallways swarmed with kids. Strangers. Moving in clumps mostly. Laughing and chatting, threading their way effortlessly around other clumps of students.

Anxiously we gazed at class lists on the bulletin board. "Hey, we're in the same class, Keri," Jennifer said. "And look! Diane, and Ron . . ."

"But I'm not," moaned Linda Evans, moving her finger down the lists. "Gee, nobody from Rosewood is in my class. And how come Gerald Stevens is in with you guys, and he doesn't even go on the same bus?"

Like a little herd of frightened calves, we clung together, trying to find our classrooms. It took us three wrong hallways to locate Linda's homeroom. We wished her luck and moved on, happy to find our classroom just two doors away. Many kids were already in the room, chatting cheerfully, sliding chosen desks along the glossy floor so each could be seated beside best friends.

"Hey, let's claim some desks too," said Ron.

Jennifer nodded. "Great idea. Diane, you can sit with us, OK?"

Within a few minutes the bell rang and a tall thin man strode into the room. Something about the way he looked at us made even the whispering stop. "I'm Mr. Korban, your homeroom teacher. And I'll be teaching you math." He spoke firmly, but his eyes sparkled behind dark brown horn-rimmed glasses, terribly out-of-style glasses. Somehow it didn't seem to matter on him.

Mr. Korban spoke about what he expected from us, and what we could expect from him. He handed out our timetables. We filled in forms, and I started to relax a bit, feeling secure in the classroom routine. Then Mr. Korban said, "Now, let's have you introduce yourselves. Tell us in one sentence a little bit about you."

Most of the class spoke so confidently, especially Ron. "I'm Ron Vander. Me and my old man farm together, and in our spare time we fix up motorcycles."

"*My dad and I* farm together," Mr. Korban corrected him.

"You and your old man farm too, eh?" Ron asked with a grin, and the class roared with laughter. I was surprised that Mr. Korban laughed too.

"Your turn." Mr. Korban nodded at the new guy from Mrs. Martin's place.

"I'm Steve Lomar. I like skiing. I really like horses, too, but I don't have one."

"That's two sentences," bellowed Ron.

Steve turned red. Mr. Korban glared at Ron. "Next, please."

"My name is Diane Spalding. We just moved here from Toronto."

Soon it was my turn. "I'm Keri Andersen," I heard myself say, "and I like reading books and riding horses."

"Except when they run," Diane whispered loudly to Jennifer. Jennifer giggled awkwardly, then glanced back, met the pain in my eyes, and looked away quickly, her cheeks red.

When we were going to our next class, Richard Simpson asked, "Hey, Diane, how come Keri doesn't like riding horses when they run? Don't tell me she's scared."

"You bet she is. She wouldn't even try to rescue me when

her little sister's horse was running away." Some of the other kids were listening now. I walked on, my face burning.

Richard said, "Oh, yeah? Tell us more."

Diane didn't need much encouragement. "Keri's chicken about lots of things. Once when we were kids, she climbed a tree and panicked, so her dad had to get a ladder and rescue her, just like a scared cat."

"Scaredy-cat," Richard said, laughing coarsely.

The only good part of it all was that Jennifer had been walking ahead with Natalie Rogers, and from the way they were chatting together, I could tell that she hadn't heard. But for sure Diane would tell her sometime.

The rest of the day dragged on. Our teachers introduced themselves, handed out booklists, and preached sermons about what they expected of us.

The school day finally ended, but the bus ride home was worse. Diane asked Jennifer to sit beside her, and she did, avoiding my eyes. The only seat left was beside one of the older girls who totally ignored me.

No one called out "Bye, Keri," when I got off the bus that afternoon.

To make my day complete, when I got home, Dad already had Fancy saddled for his own kind of teach-Keri-to-canter session.

For the first time I found myself wishing that I didn't have a horse.

Chapter 4

"We'll go to the corral to try," Dad said. "Then you won't be worried that Fancy might run away with you."

I followed him to the corral, trying desperately to think of how I could get out of this. If only *I* could understand my fear, the nameless, out-of-control feeling that choked me, then maybe I could explain it to Dad. But all I could say was "Couldn't we wait for another day? Please."

He didn't even answer, just closed the corral gate, locking us inside, then boosted me up on Fancy.

He looked at me, his face determined. "Now, walk her to the other side. Then loop your reins around the saddle horn, hang on tight with both hands, and canter back to me. She'll stop on her own when she gets here."

"What if she runs into the corral rails and crashes me with her?"

Dad let out a tight exasperated sigh. "Don't be stupid. She's not going to crash into the rails. Get off. I'll show you."

I climbed down. He lengthened the stirrups and vaulted

into the saddle. Feeling his impatience, Fancy trotted briskly across the corral. He draped the knotted reins over the horn. "Now watch." Dad sat relaxed with both hands on the horn, as Fancy loped back, and sure enough, she did come to a gentle stop on her own near the rails.

"See, nothing to worry about. Now you do it."

"But with me she might not stop." I shouldn't have said that.

"Keri!" The muscles in Dad's cheeks tightened, and I didn't dare say another word.

He jumped off Fancy, and boosted me up again. Trembling, I walked her across the corral, took a deep breath, then squeezed with my legs. She broke into a fast trot. "Stop her," shouted Dad. "Turn her around. Make her canter."

By now I was gasping. Again I faced Dad across the corral, my knuckles clenched white around the horn. "Go on, kick her. Hurry up."

I kicked her, and she broke into a canter all right, but my stupid hands left the horn to pull the reins, and then I felt myself sliding. Down, down . . .

I lay half-submerged in greasy cow manure, too angry and frustrated to cry. "Keri?" I could hear Dad's rubber boots flopping as he ran across the corral to me. "Are you OK?"

"Yes," I hissed, spitting out manure.

He bent over me. "If you're not hurt, you should get back on and try again right away. Otherwise you'll be much more frightened next time."

After such an awful day at school, the thought of falling again into that sticky manure was unbearable. I shoved away Dad's outstretched hand, struggled to my feet, and strode to the house, fuming, as he worried along beside me.

"What on earth?" Mom screeched when her slimy brown daughter appeared at the kitchen door. Up the stairs I tramped, and tried to yank clean clothes out of my dresser, but everything I touched turned mucky brown. I ran into the bathroom, washed the manure coating off my hands, then raced back to my room. I managed to find some clothes in my drawer that were still clean, scooped them up, and held them as far as possible from my filthy body while I descended two flights of stairs to the basement shower.

Mom and Dad were arguing with each other as I strode past. I could still hear them as I peeled off the smelly gooey clothes. Stepping under the comforting roar of the shower was like entering my own private world. I could have cried with relief.

They hated when I took long showers, because our forty-year-old pump might burn out. Like the summer years ago when Mr. Hanson's wife had just died, and he left the water running too long on his flower beds, burned out his pump, and had to be without water for a week. Mr. Hanson. Mr. Hanson and his little white pony . . .

Pulling on my clean clothes, I decided to pay Mr. Hanson a visit.

Mom and Dad were still arguing about what to do with their difficult daughter when I reappeared. "I'm going for a bike ride," I announced, and left them standing, too shocked to say no.

The bike swayed and spun on the gravel as I rode, pushed on by my desperation. I seemed to fly the three kilometres to Mr. Hanson's place. He was in his yard stapling old rusty wire back onto rickety fence posts.

"Hi, Keri, how are you?" He smiled. "Cows tore down the fence this afternoon. Guess they couldn't resist nice fresh garden produce." I looked across the ravaged vegetables, and wondered why he never seemed to get mad.

"How's school?"

"OK, I guess."

He leaned against a post. "What can I do for you today?"

"Well . . ." I hesitated, then took a deep breath, still tasting manure. "It's about Sandy."

"Sandy? My sweet Sandy?" He squinted, and used the hammer to push his cap up away from his sweat-covered face.

"I was wondering if I could borrow her for a while. I'd take really good care of her."

"Having some little kids coming to visit, are you? Sure, it would be all right, I guess. How long will they be at your place?"

Was it ever tempting to play along with that idea, to say they'd be at our place a few days on and off for a month or so. But he'd be sure to find out.

"I'm the one who wants to ride her, Mr. Hanson."

"You? Why on earth would you want to do that? You girls have that nice little horse and that great big beautiful mare. What would you want with my tiny Sandy?"

I could feel his eyes on me, gentle and receptive. My words tumbled over each other as I told him all about the frustration and humiliation and pain of the past few weeks.

When I ran out of breath and stood twisting a blade of grass, Mr. Hanson said, "Keri, let's go get your little pony."

He stopped at the barn for her green halter, the tiniest halter I'd ever seen.

Sandy whinnied and trotted towards us from the other side of the pasture. Mr. Hanson handed the halter to me. I put it on her, scarcely able to believe how small she was close up. Her back reached only to my waist, so much shorter than Pony Bill, and about a millionth the height of Fancy, it seemed. "Gee, Mr. Hanson, I guess she *is* too small for me, like Dad says. How many hands high is she?"

"Only eleven hands high, but she's strong and willing. I'll be betting that you'll learn to gallop on her."

Eleven hands high. Just one hundred and ten centimetres. Pony Bill was fourteen hands high, and Fancy measured sixteen. I knew I would look crazy on such a tiny horse. But I put my arms around her silky white neck, and her tiny triangular ears flipped back and forth as I talked to her.

"You really wouldn't mind if I borrowed her for a while?"

"I'm happy that someone wants to ride her. She gets so fat and bored in the pasture. My grandchildren hardly ever come from Calgary any more to ride her. I guess they've outgrown her."

I winced. His grandchildren were little kids. Mr. Hanson put his big leathery hand on Sandy's neck beside my hand. "Keri, I didn't mean it that way. They just *think* they've outgrown her. And they've got other interests too. They're too citified to come out to their old grandpa's farm to ride."

He hesitated and smiled awkwardly. "Please take her. She'll really appreciate the attention. I know you'll learn to canter on her. It's a great idea to borrow Sandy. Just as long as you don't ask to buy her." He smiled. "Because this little horse ain't ever for sale. But you tell your parents that I'd like you to keep Sandy for a while so she could get some exercise."

"I still don't think they'll let me do this. I've tried so many times to talk them into it."

He smiled mischievously. "Don't talk. Just take her home with you right now. It's hard for anybody to say no with a face like sweet Sandy's starin' them in the eyes."

"I can't take her home right now. Remember, I rode my bike."

He stroked Sandy's neck. " 'Course I remember. You just ride your bike home, leading her along behind you."

I looked at the little white horse. "She'll do that?"

"Keri, this pony will do anything for you."

She did trot behind the bike, with the rope so loose that I could have imagined she wasn't there. Her small grey nose bobbed, her long thick white mane waved in rhythm to the beat of those tiny hooves.

All the way home I pleaded, "Please, dear God, they've got to let me keep her. Please, dear God. Please."

As I turned into our gate, Dad strode out to meet me, his hands on his hips, hard lines chiselled into his face.

Chapter 5

"Keri Marie Andersen!"

"But, Dad. Mr. Hanson said he wants Sandy to get some exercise. He thought it was a good idea for me to borrow her. I'll learn to gallop on her. She's so little I won't be scared. And then I'll try on Fancy."

He still looked furious, but I couldn't give up.

"I know she's way too small for me. But Mr. Hanson said she's strong and willing. And I will learn to gallop on Fancy a lot easier if I can just get used to it first on Sandy."

He still didn't look pleased, but the straight angry line of his mouth had started to relax a tiny bit. "Please, Dad. Just let me try."

"Keri, sometimes I really wonder what's wrong with you!" I felt as though he had hit me.

He seemed to realize how much that hurt, because he immediately looked sorry. He stroked Sandy's flat broad back. "And I don't know what's wrong with me either. But

I guess I'll let you try this crazy idea." Then he turned and walked to the house.

I wanted to canter on her right away. But it was soon supper time, and then there would be dishes and chores. Most of all I didn't want to take any chance that something else could go wrong today. Maybe it wouldn't be as easy as I thought to canter on Sandy. What if I fell off her too? I needed this awful day to end happily. I'd better not try cantering tonight. First day of school, first day with a new little horse. Surely that was enough for one day.

As I led Sandy to the barn, I heard the kitchen screen door screech open and slam shut. That would be Colleen. She came running behind me. "Keri, how on earth did you do it? How did you convince Dad to let her stay?"

"Prayed real hard."

She looked at me through narrowed eyes, still puzzled. "Dad said you're to leave her in the corral tonight to give the other horses a chance to sniff her through the fence so they can't kick her or bite her. That way they'll get to know her before she goes into the pasture with them. She's so little they might beat her up." Colleen patted Sandy. "Gee, she's tiny. But she's sure pretty, eh?"

"She sure is."

"Bet I can get on her bareback without a boost," Colleen said. She gave a little jump, and sure enough, easily pulled herself up onto Sandy. "Gee, it's just like sitting on a table!" Colleen giggled as she stroked Sandy's flat wide back, and leaned over to hug her around the neck.

I felt jealous. I should have been the first one on her. "Let me try, Colleen. After all, I'm the one who brought her home, you know. You always have to butt in on everything."

"Sorry." She jumped off, her smile gone.

Why had I ruined the happy mood? "I'm sorry, Col, it's OK."

"Go on." She smiled again. "You get on her."

Without any trouble I jumped on her by myself. "She sure is little," I said, my legs dangling, almost touching the barn floor. "I shouldn't be scared to gallop on her. I could just step off if things go wrong." We laughed together. It felt so good to laugh.

The next morning I yawned a lot. It had been hard to sleep, being so excited. Now, to just get through the school day.

I hardly dared hope that Jennifer would let me sit beside her, but when I got on the bus, she met my eyes, glanced away, then slowly slid over without smiling. "Thanks," I said. "How are you?"

"OK," she said, her face relaxing a bit.

"What do you think of our teachers?" I asked.

"Miss Phillips is gorgeous." She finally smiled. "And I like Mr. Korban too." Then she looked serious. "But I sure don't like Mr. Fisher. I bet he's really mean. Not just strict. Mean. You can tell."

We were at Diane's place now. As usual, Diane was wearing *the* latest style, fresh from Toronto. I looked at my ordinary old jeans that Mom had bought on sale last spring at some department store. But I had sweet little Sandy at home, and that was better than any style of clothes.

Diane sat in front of Jennifer and me, beside Linda. They chattered happily all the way to school. I didn't say much.

It seemed to work that way all morning. Whenever Jennifer and I had a minute alone together in the hallway, Diane came bouncing along. By lunch time I couldn't stand being a third wheel any longer, so I said I had to check on something in my locker. Neither Jennifer nor Diane offered to go with me. I wandered back to the classroom with a book I had started the night before.

There sat Steve, his long lean body propped up on the ledge by the windows. He was reading a book. Those huge brown eyes looked up shyly, and a smile spread slowly across his face. It seemed to light up the whole room. "Hi, Keri."

"Do you like to read too?" I asked, hardly able to believe that a guy would sit in a classroom at lunch time reading a book. Especially a great-looking guy like Steve.

"Yeah, I love to read." He looked at the book in my hand.

"Hey, Keri, I've read that one. It's a super good horse story. Bet you'll like it." He glanced out the window at the kids strolling back to school. The bell was going to ring soon. "You're lucky to have horses. I wonder if I'll ever get to have a horse. With us buying this acreage, there won't be any extra money for a long time."

"You could ride our horses."

"I don't know how to ride. Never even tried it. Maybe you could teach me."

"Ha!" The voice shot across the empty room like a bullet. I turned to see Diane, standing with Jennifer in the doorway. "Teach you?" Diane laughed harshly. "Keri is the original coward. She's had her horse for months and can't canter." She laughed again. "She's such a wimp she won't even try."

Steve looked embarrassed and said nothing. The bell rang and the kids flocked into the room for our math class. I slumped in my desk and had an awful time concentrating on even the easiest algebra questions.

Our next class was social studies with Mr. Fisher. Social had always been one of my favourite subjects. But as we walked down the hall, we saw Mr. Fisher by the door, scowling, his arms folded across his chest as he rocked impatiently on his heels.

While we were getting seated, he puffed up his perfectly knotted tie, stretched out his arms to make his shirt sleeves sit just right inside his tweed jacket, and continued rocking on his heels.

"I expect you all to be seated much more promptly from now on. I do not tolerate tardiness or tomfoolery. Ever. Now, here's your first worksheet. It's on chapter one in your text. Get busy and read the chapter first."

As we were reading, he handed out the worksheets. I glanced at the questions. Not too exciting, I thought, and could see that the others were thinking the same thing. All the questions on his worksheet required filling in blanks. Nothing but facts and figures. There wasn't going to be much chance for creative thinking with this teacher.

At last it was time for Miss Phillips's class. Language Arts. My very favourite subject. It was considered square to like any subject, but I couldn't help it. I loved anything to do with books and reading. Miss Phillips made me a bit nervous with her poised manners, her layers of make-up, and her glamorous fashions, but I still hoped she'd be OK.

Miss Phillips walked around the room studying us. "You will be required to do one book report every month." The kids from Rosewood suppressed smiles and glanced sideways at Gerald Stevens. Gerald was the best-looking guy in the school, and probably the smoothest. At Rosewood, it had been general knowledge that he had never read a whole book in his life. It was also general knowledge that he made up every one of his book reports. I mean, really made it up. He invented the book, the plot, the characters, the author, everything. And he wrote a completely believable report.

Gerald Stevens had been doing this through all his years of school. Never once had he been caught. In fact, he usually got a very good mark on his book reports.

None of us dared tell on Gerald. He was just too popular. Besides, it was almost a class joke.

Miss Phillips had finished talking about the book reports. "And here's another assignment. Next Thursday you'll each give a four-minute talk. You can choose any subject. However, it should be something about which you are already well-acquainted, and I expect you to bring things to illustrate your talk. For example, if you are talking about gardening, you could bring various seeds, gardening tools . . ."

"A dirty shovel," Ron Vander snickered. Miss Phillips scowled at him.

"Small *clean* garden tools," she continued, "actual samples of garden plants and weeds, labels from fertilizers or weed sprays, and so on."

What topic could I pick, I wondered, gazing out the window, watching heavy grey clouds churning, thick and threatening. I sure hoped it wouldn't rain this afternoon.

But it did. After school I slopped through the mud in my

new running shoes and climbed on the bus, shaking the water from my hair.

Jennifer and Diane were sitting together. I sat across from them and smiled faintly. "Kinda wet, eh?"

"Yeah," Jennifer answered, barely turning to look at me as she continued telling Diane about Gerald's made-up book reports. They laughed and kidded as though they'd known each other for years.

But that wasn't as bad as the rain. I listened to the rhythmic groan of the window wipers slopping rain off the bus windows.

No riding Sandy today.

When I got home, I trudged upstairs to my bedroom and lay on my back with my head hanging down over the edge of the bed. It seemed a relaxing way to lie, and always felt good with the blood pooling in my brain. Only trouble was that the pictures on my wall always looked upside down that way. I had lots of good horse pictures covering the wall, but it seemed a shame to spend most of the time seeing them the wrong way up.

Then I got a brainwave. Why not turn some of the pictures on that wall upside down? It might look funny to someone else, but it was my bedroom, and I spent so much time lying that way that I might as well enjoy the pictures my way too.

By the time I finished rearranging, it was supper time, but still raining hard.

For the rest of the week it poured. Dad and Mom were worried about our barley swaths lying out in the fields getting spoiled in the rain, the kids at school were getting squirrelly from being indoors, and the teachers were getting cranky. But worst for me was that I still hadn't been able to try cantering on Sandy. Each day after school I put on my slicker and rubber boots and led Sandy into the barn to talk to her. I couldn't even brush her very well because she was so wet.

Fancy always whinnied to be fussed over too, but I left her out in the rain with water pouring off her nose. She seemed so big now. Besides, I needed to make Sandy feel at home, feel that I was her friend.

I spent a lot of time in the barn. Reading didn't seem to appeal to me as it usually did on rainy days. I thought of my four-minute talk. What subject could I pick? It was Friday now.

Almost all the kids had chosen a topic. Ron, of course, was doing motorcycles. "What're you going to bring?" asked the kids. "Your motorbike?"

"Naw. I don't think Phillips would appreciate that enough to make it worthwhile." We all laughed.

"Hey, Gerald," cooed Natalie Rogers, sidling up to him, "how come you won't tell anybody what your topic is?"

"Yeah, come on, tell us," Diane coaxed.

"You'll see."

"Ha," Ron said, clearly unimpressed. "He ain't telling 'cause he don't know yet."

Gerald glared at Ron. "I do so, Vander. And it's going to be a lot better than motorcycles, I'll tell you that."

"When's it ever going to stop raining?" I asked Dad that evening.

"Pretty soon, I hope." He sighed deeply. "You know it always seems to rain when it's harvest time."

When I awoke the next morning I could not hear the sound of rain. The glorious chirping of birds pushed my brain into full gear. And sunshine painted my bedroom golden.

Chapter 6

Saturday and sunshine!

Ernie and Patches had milk replacer shoved under their noses and yanked away the minute they started to make foam in the bottom of the pails. Eggs were gathered so fast that the hens didn't have time to peck my hands. My room received what Grandma would have called "a lick and a promise." Dust got smeared off the furniture in the living room, and the vacuum roared as I jerked it back and forth over the carpet.

After lunch Dad went to town for some machine parts. I did dishes while Mom and Colleen went to our swamp of a garden to dig carrots and potatoes for supper.

They dumped the vegetables on the lawn and turned on the hose to squirt off the mud. I couldn't wait any longer. "Mom, when can I go riding?"

She laughed. "How about right now?"

"Me too?" asked Colleen.

"Nope. First you finish cleaning these carrots and potatoes.

We can sit out here in the sunshine and scrub them so they'll be ready to cook for supper. Keri did a lot more work than you did this morning."

Colleen said nothing. I knew she wished I would offer to help with the vegetables, but I just put on my boots, said, "Thanks, Mom," and went to get Sandy.

All three horses trotted through the mud to meet me. I wrapped my arms around Sandy. Fancy rubbed her head against my arm, trying to get some attention, but Sandy started to move away, so I pushed Fancy back. Really jealous now, Fancy charged Sandy, her ears flattened against her neck, her teeth bared. I watched, terrified that Fancy was going to kill my tiny friend.

But Sandy made the craziest sound, a loud, rhythmic, squealing grunt, like a pig, and that tiny pony backed up and kicked Fancy in the shoulder. Fancy stopped, shocked, then laid her ears back and charged again. Sandy repeated her squeaky grunt and kicked again. Fancy spun around and hammered Sandy with both back feet. But Sandy just grunted and squealed louder, striking Fancy with her hind feet, over and over again, until that great big horse backed off and stood staring meekly down at her.

I watched the encounter, amazed. It was like David and Goliath. Oh, why couldn't I be courageous like Sandy or David, or even Colleen? Are all the little ones brave? Maybe they needed to be brave to survive. What did they have that I didn't have?

Mom and Colleen came running.

"What's going on?" asked Mom. "We heard the strangest noise. Like a pig. Real loud."

"It was Sandy. Showing Fancy that she can't push her around."

"Sandy?" Both Mom and Colleen looked sceptical. "Keri, this was the noise like a pig would make. A squeally grunt. Uuuuh Uuuuh Uuuuh." Mom laughed as she tried to imitate the sound, and then when I nodded, she laughed harder. "Sandy? Really?"

Then she looked at Colleen. "Now that we're here, you might as well get Pony Bill in. I'll finish the vegetables later."

Colleen's eyes lit up. "Thanks, Mom."

When I put my saddle on Sandy, I could hardly believe how silly it looked. I couldn't help laughing. "Saddle's bigger than the horse."

Mom chuckled. "I was thinking that too, but I didn't want to say it." She put her head down to Sandy's soft puffy white mane.

"Keri, do you want help tightening the cinch?"

"Naw. She's so short, it's easy."

Mom helped Colleen tighten Pony Bill's cinch, and then stood back watching Sandy and me with a strange sad look on her face.

I put my foot into the stirrup, expecting to vault easily onto Sandy, but instead the saddle swung down, almost underneath her. "Ah, she blows her tummy up," Colleen said, while I stood with one foot still caught up in the stirrup.

Mom tightened the cinch this time, but still the saddle slipped when I tried to get up. Again she tried, pulling the cinch until her face turned red. Sandy struggled to keep her balance, spreading her tiny hooves as wide apart as possible. "The trouble," Mom said, groaning between pulls, "is not just that she's so fat. It's the flatness of her back. Like a table. The saddle doesn't sit very well on it."

Eventually Mom got the cinch so tight that Sandy's fat bulged around both sides, like a lumpy lady in a girdle. At last we were ready.

I climbed on and looked at the ground. Close. Real close. It wouldn't be far to fall, that was for sure.

As Colleen and I rode down the lane, I wondered when I should try to canter. Maybe it shouldn't be today. Maybe I should get used to Sandy's walking and trotting first, get to know her better. Even at a walk, riding her was a completely new experience. The way the saddle rocked with her short brisk steps, the way she handled . . . The reins were about half the length on Sandy's short fat neck as on Fancy's long slender neck. And compared with Fancy's long leisurely strides, Sandy's legs blurred in a staccato.

For me to look up at Colleen on Pony Bill was a strange feeling too. I laughed nervously. "Sure hope nobody sees me."

After a few peaceful minutes of walking, I said, "Let's trot."

Sandy's trot was surprisingly comfortable. Not rough like Pony Bill's, even though her legs were shorter. She was unbelievably gentle and calm. And, oh, so close to the ground. A feeling of peace spread through me and I felt that I really could learn to canter. On this horse I would try and I would succeed.

But when? Not tomorrow, not next week. Today. It was one of those autumn days that made my soul sing. Blue sky, mellow sunshine, the smell of ripe grain, and a few wild rose bushes already blazing red, orange, and gold.

Why not make this day absolutely perfect? "Colleen, let's canter," I heard myself saying as though from far away, but my heart was pounding with anticipation.

"Sure thing." She smiled at me. Then she looked toward the road, and her smile dissolved. "Oh-oh."

It was Diane, riding her bike towards us. Colleen asked gently, "Are you ready for this?"

Chapter 7

"What on earth are you doing, Keri?" Diane shrilled, stopping her bike beside us. "The SPCA would have you arrested. Poor pony, you'll break its back." She laughed loudly. "What's happened to Fancy?"

"Nothing."

"So how come you're dragging your feet on this poor little thing?" She laughed again, a raw harsh cackle. "Just wait till the kids hear about this on Monday."

"Look, what do you want, Diane?" asked Colleen. "You must have come over here for some reason other than to make fun of Keri."

I could have hugged my sister. Where did she get her nerve?

Undaunted, Diane continued her sarcasm. "Actually, Mom sent me over to spend the afternoon with Keri. But she doesn't know that Keri's gone back to her babyhood. Bad enough to be a coward, but this is ridiculous."

"Would you like to come horseback riding with us?" Sugarsweetness coated Colleen's voice. "We've saved Fancy for you to ride."

"No thanks." Diane turned her bike around. "I've got better things to do. Like maybe play with my dollies," she yelled over her shoulder.

I watched Diane pedal back down the long lane and disappear as she turned onto the road. "Thanks, Col."

"Oh, she makes me sick. What do you want to do now?"

"Canter," I said, still so angry my throat burned. I held Sandy's reins with one hand, and grabbed the horn with the other. I took a deep breath, looked at the soft grass along the lane, and touched my heels to her sides.

Sandy started to canter. Oh, she was plenty fast, the ground skimmed beside us, but I was staying on. Her strong little shoulders lifted and fell, lifted and fell. Her hoofs beat softly along the edge of the lane, her tiny ears pointed forward. She seemed to be enjoying herself. I couldn't say the same for me, but it wasn't too bad either. Not at all like on Fancy. Not that terrible feeling of height and speed and too much power.

Pony Bill was running beside Sandy, with Colleen shouting, "You're doing it! You're cantering!"

Why is it that when people are really happy, they cry? Tears blurred my eyes, and choked my throat. After a while my muscles began to relax. By the time we reached the end of the lane, I felt almost reluctant to pull Sandy to a stop.

Colleen started to cry too. "This is stupid," she said, rubbing her horse-dirty hands across her face, smearing her tears into mud.

I began to laugh through my tears. "I did it, Col. I did it. And I'll learn on Fancy too."

Then I thought of myself sixteen hands above the ground. "Well, I'll practise on Sandy for a while. Col, you know, it's heights that scare me more than anything else."

We turned the horses. "Let's try again," I said. Both of the horses started to run, much faster than before, eager to get home. I yanked Sandy to a walk, afraid again, disgusted with myself.

"Let's walk them back to the yard, and then canter *away* from home," suggested Colleen.

I nodded.

That worked better. This time we went the full length of the lane. It seemed a long way and my legs were aching, but I shouted. "Hey, this is fun. It's really fun."

After a couple more times, I noticed Mom standing in the yard with her hands on her hips, beaming. We galloped back to her, and that was fast and very scary. I gripped one hand tight around the horn, but didn't pull back on the reins this time.

We stopped in front of Mom. I was puffing almost as much as Sandy. "Mom, I did it! I did it!"

"I know!" It had been so long since she had sounded proud of me. "Dad will be back from town pretty soon, so don't take the saddles off the horses. I want him to see this."

While we were talking, we heard the truck coming down the lane. "There's Dad!" said Colleen. "Let's go!"

I followed at a gallop, grinning so hard my cheeks hurt. When Dad saw us he braked immediately and sat smiling.

"What's this I see?" he said, as we stopped beside him.

He got out of the truck, put his arm around Sandy's sweaty neck, and hugged her. "Well, little Sandy, I guess it was a good idea to borrow you after all. You taught my Skalawag that she can do something that she's scared of."

"Oh, Dad, it's so much easier on Sandy than on Fancy. I love Sandy so much. I wish we could buy her and I could always ride her."

His eyes narrowed and that little muscle tightened on the side of his cheek. "You can't ride Sandy forever. Don't get too used to her, or you'll be even more afraid of a horse that's the right size for you."

He must have seen my face. He rubbed my hair, laughing gently, and said, "Skalawag, you can keep Sandy a little while longer. Just don't wear out your boots dragging them on the ground."

Back in the barn I brushed Sandy and hugged her and talked to her. Matilda rubbed my legs, begging for attention. Just for fun, I put her on Sandy, expecting her to jump right down again. But she didn't. She continued purring, and snuggled happily on Sandy's soft table-top back. Sandy didn't seem to mind.

"Hey, Keri, lead Sandy around. See if Matilda can ride a horse."

She could. We led Sandy, turned her, even trotted her, but Matilda rode proudly. Ever since she was a tiny kitten, Matilda had ridden in my bike basket, and she loved riding in the truck, but this seemed to be her real calling. A cat cowgirl.

After a while we went back to the barn, and I pulled Matilda off so I could brush Sandy some more. Matilda jumped back on.

All too soon it was time for supper. We let the horses free in the pasture and laughed as Sandy followed Pony Bill to the dirt hole, worn deep from months of rolling. She stood waiting as his knees collapsed and he rocked on his back, groaning with pleasure, his legs pumping in the air. When he got up, shaking off the loose dirt, Sandy took her turn. Fancy hadn't been ridden, but she had to have a roll too. We laughed harder.

"Funny how they never roll on grass," I said.

Colleen giggled. "I guess they like being dirty."

After supper dishes, I hurried back to Sandy. She walked towards me, nickering softly. I hugged her, then decided to sit on her bareback with no rope or halter. That's dangerous, a little voice seemed to say. But I answered out loud. "I can easily jump off, she's so close to the ground."

Just a slight jump and my body folded over her back, then another little jump and my leg swung over the other side. I sat there, and nothing happened. Absolutely nothing. Sandy stood with her head up for a minute, then started eating grass.

Wrapping my arms around her neck, I pushed my face into her silky mane and lay with my feet up, crossed over her rump. Happiness. She continued grazing, flicking her ears back and forth as I told her of my fears and problems, told her how I loved her. Once in a while she turned her head back to touch my arm with her velvety grey nose.

If only I could persuade Mr. Hanson to sell Sandy. But how could I ever convince Mom and Dad that we should buy such a small horse? Why, oh why, couldn't she be bigger? But that was a stupid wish; it was her tiny size that had given me confidence.

If only she could grow a tiny bit every day from now on as I got used to galloping, I thought, so that soon she would be tall without my even noticing it.

Or, if only I could be smaller.

But I could never be smaller, she could never be bigger, and somehow I would have to convince my parents that it was right for me to continue riding her and maybe even to buy her. "Sweet Sandy." I hugged her tightly. "Sweet Sandy, somehow, someday, you're going to be mine."

Chapter 8

The next afternoon we galloped west, planning to visit Mr. Hanson. As we approached Mrs. Martin's old place, Colleen asked, "Do you want to ride in and say hi to the new neighbours?"

"Naw. Steve might make fun of Sandy just like Diane."

"I doubt it."

He was in the garden and waved at us to come into the yard. "No choice," whispered Colleen.

"That's a cute pony," Steve said, stroking Sandy's face.

"She's kinda small for me. She belongs to Mr. Hanson a couple of miles west of here."

"Yeah, I thought you had a big brown mare." He looked puzzled.

I figured I'd better tell him the truth. "I borrowed this pony because I was scared to canter, just like Diane told you. Sandy's so tiny, I thought it wouldn't be so scary as on my big horse. And it worked. Yesterday I did gallop on her, and now it seems almost fun."

Steve laughed, but there was no mocking or scorn in his voice. Just friendliness and fun. "Sounds like a good idea. How much longer can you keep her?"

"Dad says just a little while more. Then I have to try cantering on Fancy before I get too used to Sandy's size."

"It must be fun to ride a horse even at a walk."

Colleen looked up at him. "Why not come riding with us this afternoon?" Her nerve never ceased to amaze me.

"Do you mean it?"

"Of course," said Colleen. "You could ride Fancy."

He beamed. "Come on in and meet my parents. I'll just check with them."

How strange to see someone else's furniture in Mrs. Martin's house and to talk to new people there. Steve introduced us to his father, a small quiet man with a gentle smile, and to his mother, a tall thick woman with a friendly booming voice.

"Come on in," Mrs. Lomar said. "Have a glass of juice and a piece of chocolate cake. I just baked it. Keri and Colleen Andersen, eh? So you're the girls who live just east of here. Sure was nice of you to ride over for a visit. Cindy! Come meet our company."

A little girl appeared from what used to be Mrs. Martin's sewing room. She looked shyly at us, winding a braid around her finger. "Hi."

"Cindy's going to be starting school next year. Cindy, meet our new friends. Keri, you're in Steven's class, aren't you?"

How did she know that? Had Steve been talking about me? And if so, why?

The juice was refreshing, the cake delicious. It didn't take much to persuade us to devour a second piece. But I could see that Steve was anxious to get going.

Mom looked surprised to see a guy bicycling beside us into the yard. She greeted him warmly and then helped saddle Fancy for him to ride.

Steve scratched Fancy's face, and looked at us, beaming.

"When I woke up this morning, I had a funny feeling that something great was going to happen today."

Within a few minutes Steve had mastered the art of steering a horse, and was trotting Fancy around the yard, his lanky body totally relaxed, as though he had balanced in a saddle for years. It felt good to see somebody so happy.

We went for a ride along the road, Colleen on Pony Bill of course, and Steve towering above me on Fancy.

"Aren't you scared to be up so high?" I finally dared to ask him.

"No. I love it. It's exciting."

"I wish I were brave like you."

"But I'm not really being brave if I do something I'm not scared of. You're scared and you try it anyway, so you're being brave."

"Brave? Steve, you don't know me. I've been a wimp all my life." The way he was listening made it so easy to talk. "When I was little I was even scared to get into bed because I thought there were bears under my bed that would slash my ankles with their claws and bite my legs with their terrible teeth. I was so scared that I jumped into bed from way far back so the bears couldn't reach me."

"But you did get in," Steve persisted. "Somebody who isn't scared of bears under his bed wouldn't be brave even if he stood with his toes right underneath. If you were scared, and you still jumped, then you were being brave."

Colleen nodded. "He's right, Keri."

I laughed, a mocking laugh. "Here I am riding a pony so little that my legs drag, because I'm scared stiff to canter on Fancy, and you guys are trying to tell me I'm brave."

Steve looked down at me with such gentleness that my heart thumped. "You'll canter on Fancy someday. I know you will. You'll still be afraid until you get used to it, but you'll do it anyway."

The horses' hooves beat softly along the edge of the road. The sun felt good after all the days of chilly autumn rain. A flock of geese honked their way through the sapphire sky.

"How are you getting along with your report for Thursday?" asked Steve.

"Not too well."

"What topic have you picked?"

"I haven't picked a topic yet. That's the problem. I don't know what I want to talk about."

"Horses," Colleen said. "Why don't you talk about horses?"

"Great idea," Steve said. "Why not?"

"Oh sure." I laughed. "I could bring Sandy to class."

Colleen and Steve laughed with me.

"Seriously," Steve continued, "there're lots of things you could bring. Almost all the kids in our class are city kids, and many of them have never seen a bridle or a horseshoe or anything like that. Just in pictures. I bet they'd find it interesting."

"What are you going to talk about, Steve?" asked Colleen. I wished I'd been the one to ask.

"Aluminum."

"Aluminum?" we chimed.

"Yep, aluminum. We visited my uncle in Kitimat, B.C., last summer, and he took us to the smelting plant where aluminum is made from bauxite. You should see it! Huge cauldrons of molten metal ore, glowing orange! They add cryolite to bring its melting point down to *only* 2000 degrees. They use so much electricity that anywhere nearby you can get paper clips to hang together and stand up on end . . ."

Even Colleen was listening with real interest. I could tell that Steve's topic was going to be a winner.

Back in my room that night I found it difficult to concentrate on my talk. I could discuss the care of horses, riding . . . But if I spoke about things like that, Diane would be sure to make sarcastic remarks about my own riding abilities.

I was lying on my back as usual, with my head flopped over the edge of my bed, looking at the upside down pictures of horses, when I got an idea. Why not talk about horses like a biologist would talk about any animal? I could describe their eyesight, digestion, habits, special adaptations for survival, all those naturalist kind of things.

But then what could I bring to show? Obviously halters and bridles and brushes wouldn't fit in with that kind of talk. I'd read many nature books. They always discussed the animal's coat, tracks, teeth, even the scat, which is the fancy naturalist term for manure.

I could bring the old horse skull that Colleen and I had found in a coulee a few miles away. That would show the teeth. And instead of tracks, I could bring hoof trimmings and could draw pictures of a horse's hoof, showing the "frog" that helps pump the blood back to the heart. They might find that interesting. As for scat . . . Of course there was lots of that around, and I could bring a couple of the hard, dried-up, round little "meadow muffins" as Mom called them, and use them to discuss the digestive system of the horse.

I spent the rest of the evening buried in our encyclopedia, learning more about the horse from a naturalist's point of view. This was going to be interesting!

Even the next morning being Monday didn't daunt my good spirits. And that afternoon in math class, I had a pleasant surprise.

When I finished my assignment, I slipped my library book out and stealthily started to read it. Usually teachers hate it when you do anything except their subjects in class, so I'd learned to hide a novel under my school work to catch little snatches of reading.

The book was wonderful, so absorbing that I didn't notice Mr. Korban standing beside me. I looked up, trapped, and slid the book under my math text, my face burning red. But Mr. Korban just smiled and bent to check my assignment. "Good," he said, then continued walking around on his quiet rubber-soled shoes, checking everybody's work, helping with problems.

After a few minutes he strolled to the blackboard. "Now, let's take up the first five questions on page three. By the way, if any of you finish your work early, feel free to read a library book or write a letter or whatever. Just as long as you don't bother anybody." He smiled again. I felt the muscles in my back and shoulders relax as if I were sitting in sunshine.

On Wednesday night I collected stuff for my report. Carefully I cut a small piece of Sandy's mane to put into a plastic bag. In another plastic bag I put a hoof clipping, and into another, a piece from one of Sandy's chestnuts, those strange, rough growths on the inside of every horse's leg. I washed the dust and cobwebs off the wonderful old horse skull, and put everything into Dad's grey duffle bag. With these props and my drawings of a horse's foot from the bottom and in cross section, I felt quite ready for my naturalist talk on the horse. There remained only the matter of the scat.

This required some thought. Would the kids think it crazy to bring horse manure to class? Yet that was one of the important things in any naturalist write-up. There was always a picture of the scat, but I certainly didn't want to draw a picture of it. An actual piece of horse dung would add credibility to my discussion of the herbivorous digestive system of the horse. It would show undigested fibre from grass or hay. The spherical shape would show the powerful peristaltic contraction of the large intestine, and a herbivore's ability to conserve water by extracting it from the intestine, resulting in a pellet-type scat similar to that of deer, elk, or rabbit.

But what would the kids think? Most of them had probably never seen horse manure. Maybe all the more reason why I should bring a sample. They wouldn't know what I was talking about if I just described it. But city kids? Maybe they'd think it was gross, without giving me a chance to show how it illustrated the points of my talk.

I changed my mind a dozen times, then into a plastic bag I placed two small, round, very dried-up manure samples with lots of undigested fibre showing. I could always decide at school, I thought.

Chapter 9

When I swung the heavy duffle bag ahead of me onto the bus the next morning, Ron yelled, "Hey Keri, whatcha got in that big bag? Mr. Hanson's pony?" I laughed, and he didn't ask any more questions. Ron held a big cardboard box on his lap. The way he carried it off the bus, I could tell it was heavy. Most of my classmates carried bags or boxes into the school that morning. You could almost touch the excitement. Miss Phillips's double period of English was going to be anything but boring.

None of us could concentrate in Mr. Fisher's social studies class that morning. Mr. Fisher never taught anything anyway; he just made us fill in worksheets. He handed out the day's sheet, and we began the tedious task of searching for answers in the designated chapter of our textbook.

As usual, Gerald was copying the answers from Roxanne Campbell, peering over her shoulder. It burned me, because the rest of us worked for our answers. I could tell it angered

Roxanne too. She tried her best to hide her work under another paper or cover it with her arm.

Roxanne had to sit in front of Gerald because of Mr. Fisher's seating plan, but why didn't she simply report his cheating? I didn't know much about Roxanne; she kept to herself a lot. From what I'd seen, she never tried to impress anybody or work her way into the tight groups. So why would she be afraid of getting Gerald Stevens mad at her? Hard to imagine Roxanne scared of anything or anyone. Yet she sat with jaw muscles clamped tight, back tensed, and didn't tell on a guy who deserved to be in trouble.

At last the recess bell rang. I sighed. Somehow, I had managed to find all the answers on that ridiculous worksheet.

Mr. Fisher roared as he collected the worksheets. "Only half done! What are you trying to prove? What's going on here?" He took mine and looked it over. "Excellent, Keri. Just excellent!"

I cringed.

After collecting all the worksheets, he stood rocking back and forth on his feet. "Keri was the only one who completed her work. Everyone else will be coming back here at noon today to finish these. Good for you, Keri, for finishing. You should be proud of yourself. The rest of you should be ashamed."

Oh groan. Just what I needed to be really popular! As we shuffled back to our lockers to get our things for Miss Phillips's class, the kids glared at me.

Locker doors slammed louder than usual, and voices were tense and tight. Mr. Fisher's class had certainly punctured the buoyant mood of earlier in the morning.

We trudged with our heavy bags into Miss Phillips's room.

"We'll go in alphabetical order . . ." the teacher started. My chest tightened because that meant I'd be second after Betty Adams. Ron Vander whistled through his teeth, and shouted, "All right!" holding his arms out and bowing.

Miss Phillips smiled sweetly at Ron. "Yes, alphabetical

order, only backwards." The class hooted and cheered. Ron groaned and screwed up his face in exaggerated pain. Even I was laughing. The awful mood from Mr. Fisher's class seemed to ebb away.

And now I'd be second from last. I could have hugged Miss Phillips. Except that would have smeared her layers of carefully applied make-up and rumpled her immaculate clothes. No, she definitely would not appreciate that, I thought, smiling, as Ron strolled to the front of the room. He set the big cardboard box on the table and started sorting through his things, pretending to grimace. He was having a ball.

"My topic is motorcycles," Ron said. "Some of you don't appreciate the finer things of life, mainly motorcycles, so I've decided that today you're all going to get your basic education."

He reached into the box and pulled out a heavy block of metal about the size of a lunch pail. "This here is the heart of the animal. And to those who insist on thinking of a motorcycle as just a machine, this would be what you'd call the engine. Well, actually, this part I'm holding here is the engine block. Now, in this cardboard box, I have all the important parts that fit into this here engine to make it work. So watch real careful."

"Carefully," said Miss Phillips.

"Huh?" Ron looked up from his engine block, baffled.

"Carefully. You said, 'Watch real careful.' You should have said 'Watch carefully.' "

"Oh, yeah," Ron said, as he turned to lift more little parts out of his box. "Right. This here's the piston and it moves up and down to give the compression—that's the power. These rings are just like your standard wedding rings—they seal things in so they can't escape."

He showed how all the other parts fit into the engine block—the valves, connecting rods, cam shaft, spark plugs, ignition coil . . .

You couldn't help but be interested in Ron's talk. In fact, even Miss Phillips seemed fascinated. "Oh, my goodness.

Ron, you've gone over your four minutes. You've had six. Sorry, Ron, but you'll have to quit. Thank you very much. Karen Sutherland, you're next."

Karen's talk was about her favourite rock group. She had one poster and two magazine pictures and told a few things about each member of the group. I noticed that Miss Phillips looked disappointed. Karen always took such care about her clothes and make-up, but obviously she hadn't spent much time or energy preparing for her talk.

"Gerald, you're next."

No amount of prodding had made Gerald divulge his topic. Now he sauntered to the front of the room, surveyed his kingdom, and announced, "My topic is telephones."

Telephones! Who would have ever guessed? Gerald did a great job of his talk. He had a telephone in pieces, and explained the function of each part. But how on earth had he managed to get so much information? It would take work to find out all these things. And it wasn't like Gerald to put effort into anything.

Ryan was next with his collection of baseball bubblegum cards, and then it was Diane's turn. She had informed us days before that she'd be talking about her two-week summer holiday in Greece. No one else in our class had even been to Europe, so Greece made a nice impressive topic. And she did a nice impressive job. Miss Phillips sat forward in her chair, smiling and nodding as Diane showed a replica of an old Greek vase, enlarged photos of the Parthenon, a painting from Crete . . .

Richard Simpson's talk was gruesome. He spoke about methods of torture throughout history. He'd been through the chamber of horrors in a wax museum, studied torture scenes in movies, collected pictures of torture methods, and even made a few models to show us the finer details.

I could hardly wait until his talk ended. My turn was coming closer. That was torture enough.

Harvey Round didn't do much to cheer us with his four minutes about weather maps. He was a homely, frail boy who always seemed to have a head cold. Sure enough, Harvey sniffed a few times, and Richard imitated each sniff, then sat looking innocent while the rest of the class tried not to laugh, and Miss Phillips glared.

Steve's discussion about aluminum went very well. He gave me a little grin as he sat down. I sat up straighter and smiled back.

With each new talk, my heart pounded louder and my mouth felt dryer. I began to wish we'd gone in regular alphabetical order. At least my speech would have been over long ago, and I would be recuperating now and maybe even enjoying myself.

Len Chan's talk was superb. He spoke of China, the land of his grandparents. He'd brought beautiful Chinese watercolour paintings, ivory and jade carvings, lacquered plates and vases. Most amazing of all, we saw an embroidery done with "Forbidden Stitch," a stitch so tiny that the women who did it eventually became blind. Over a hundred years ago an emperor had made the stitch illegal, and the embroidered picture Len showed us was about two hundred years old.

I was glad I didn't have to follow Len. Anything would have paled in comparison. But Roxanne Campbell did a good job anyway, telling us about feeding birds in winter. She'd brought samples of bird seeds, actual bird feeders, and showed which seeds and feeders attract which birds.

Her voice started out soft, so soft that I had to strain to hear, but the longer she talked, the more excited she became. I was surprised. I'd never seen Roxanne's eyes sparkle before.

"And once the birds know where you are, they'll keep coming back," Roxanne said. "You can recognize some of them year after year." There was a sound, almost a giggle in the back of her throat. "There's this one jay who's been coming to my yard for three years, and he's so fussy he won't eat anything except dried corn . . ."

She broke off suddenly, as if she had said too much, as if she realized for the first time that there were almost thirty of us watching her. Then her eyes dropped and she hurried to stuff away all the props she'd brought.

"Well, that's it, that's everything," she mumbled, before fleeing to her seat. There was an uncomfortable silence until Miss Phillips seemed to remember herself.

"Thank you, Roxanne," the teacher blurted. "Darcy Chambers?"

I lurched back to reality. It would be my turn next.

When Darcy finished talking about his two-week vacation in Honolulu, I walked with rubbery legs to the front of the room.

Chapter 10

I lifted the old horse skull from the canvas bag. "My topic is the horse, from a naturalist's point of view." At least no one was laughing. "The horse is specialized for life in the wild . . ." My mouth felt dry and sticky as though I'd been eating peanut butter directly from a jar. ". . . a life of running and grazing. Their main defence is to sense danger and to escape."

I stopped. What was it I was supposed to say next? My mind went blank. What was I talking about? Oh yes, "Horses have good hearing. Their ears rotate to pick up sound from any direction. With their large nostrils they smell dangerous things from far away. They have the biggest eyes of any land animal except ostriches."

I had almost forgotten to show the picture of the horse head. "See, their eyes are set in the side, so they can notice things behind them. Each eye can move separately, and the oval shape makes objects from behind seem to move faster, so the horse will frighten easily and run from danger."

To my amazement, the kids were all listening intently.

"Horses' legs are adapted for speed. Each hoof is really only the tip of one toe. Their real heel bone is at the top of the front leg and about half way up the back leg." I held up the hoof clipping and drawings. "The hoof wall is tough, but the frog inside is rubbery to absorb jolts.

"When wild horses aren't running, they are grazing." I pointed to the old skull. "Dust and sand on the grass would wear their teeth down, so the teeth never stop growing. The molars are flat with rough swirls on the tops for grinding grass."

Here it comes, I thought, the part about digestion. Should I or shouldn't I show the meadow muffins? "Like any other herbivore, the horse has a very long intestine and a pouch called a cecum containing bacteria to help digest the cellulose of grass. But this digestion is never complete . . ." My voice sounded squeaky. I took a deep breath. "Much undigested cellulose fibre remains. . . ." My trembling hands took the clear plastic bag containing two little horse turds. "Now, in every naturalist book, you always read about scat. . . ."

"Keri Andersen! What on earth have you got there?" Miss Phillips sounded horrified and furious. I hadn't even thought of *her* reaction.

"Miss Phillips, it's scat from the horse. It's to show the digestive system."

Some of the kids started laughing, and that made Miss Phillips even more angry. "I don't care what it's supposed to show. How dare you bring horse manure to school! Throw it in the garbage this instant." She waved her sculptured fingernails. "No, you'd better not put it in the garbage can or we'll be in trouble with the janitor. Keri, how could you?"

"But, Miss Phillips, it's old and dry and it doesn't have any smell or anything."

"Put it back in your bag, and sit down right now."

Shaking, I stuffed my things into the duffle bag, my face red-hot, my throat tight.

I heard several giggles and recognized Diane's as one of the loudest.

"Betty Adams. Your turn, please."

While Betty talked about Yellowstone National Park, I hunched in my desk, wondering how I could run away. Run away to where? Run away on the prairies. I could gallop away on Sandy. Follow the meadowlarks. But you can't hide a girl and a pony, even such a tiny pony, behind a tumbleweed. Nothing to cover you on a prairie. Nothing, nothing to hide behind.

Betty was sitting down now, and Miss Phillips was saying that tomorrow she'd tell us the marks for our talks. The bell rang and everybody went to their lockers to get their lunches. Gerald was the centre of attention; everyone wanted to know where he'd managed to get all his information about telephones. He bragged that his uncle worked for the telephone company and got all the telephone parts and made up the whole talk for him. Didn't his uncle deserve an A? All the kids were laughing as they carried their lunches back to the classroom.

"Whatcha eating, Keri?" Trevor Fowler asked. "Horse poop?" Their laughter made my stomach hurt. I sat at my desk chewing a dry cheese sandwich, my eyes too heavy to look at anything or anyone.

The voices were loud and flippant, talking about the speeches.

"I think Keri should get a special prize for what she brought," said Richard.

Diane groaned. "Guess what, you guys. Don't you remember? We're supposed to be in stupid old Fisher's room in five minutes." A knife-sharp edge came to her voice as she added, "All of us except Keri."

"Yeah," Trevor sneered, "Keri had to get her work all finished so we'd look bad, so Fisher would have to keep the rest of us in at lunch time."

Richard's eyes were livid. "Keri, the brown-nose, Mr. Fisher's pet."

"And Keri, the coward," shrilled Diane.

Sam Duncan stood up and made a mock bow towards me. "Ladies and gentlemen, I present to you, Keri, the horse turd."

I glanced around desperately. Jennifer was sitting silently, her head bent down, fidgeting with her pencil. She looked up at me, and I saw that she was almost ready to cry. She still liked me. It hit me with a jolt. She still cared.

"Maybe it's Keri that should have been put in the garbage can, not her horse poop." I couldn't believe Karen Sutherland would say something like that.

"Yeah, she's garbage." Richard's voice rose, with a new and terrifying harshness to it. "So let's put her where she belongs." He rushed for me with Trevor and Sam on his heels.

This *can't* be happening, I kept thinking, as they dragged me to the front of the room, hoisted me up, and pushed me face down inside the huge dark green metal garbage can. Richard was still gripping my shoulder and twisting my arm behind my back. But I hardly felt that pain.

A stream of tears dropped off my face into the pencil shavings and scrap paper and apple cores. I struggled to lift my head over the rim of the can, and through drowning eyes, saw Ron charge towards us. "Leave her alone, Simpson! You guys get away from her or I'll smash all your teeth in."

They let me go, scattering. Ron yanked me out of the garbage can. "You guys think you're something, eh? Well, don't bother to do nothing like that again to nobody. Ever."

No one said anything. Ron looked around, and I was surprised to see that he was shaking. His voice softened a bit. "Come on, you guys, we'd better get to Fisher's room." In silence, everyone shuffled out of the room, and I stood there alone.

They returned just before the bell rang. No one would look at me. Math class was very quiet.

At recess I tapped Ron on the back when he was getting his books out of the locker. "Ron?"

He turned around and looked at me shyly. "Yeah?"

"Thanks."

"Ah, it was nothing." He flushed pink. "Well, I guess we'd better get to French."

I walked into Mrs. Kelly's room and slumped into my desk, wondering when this horrible day would ever end.

Mrs. Kelly began her class by saying, "We're going to try something different today. I want all of you to pair up and practise the irregular verbs."

Most of the kids quickly picked a partner and moved their desks together. Natalie Rogers was sitting with Diane. No one had picked Jennifer yet. My spirits lifted a bit. I glanced at Jennifer, trying not to look too desperate. She smiled uneasily, and started to push her desk towards mine.

I let out a deep breath. Thank you, Jennifer, thank you, thank you. I noticed Harvey Round looking about with wide frantic eyes. Poor Harvey. Apart from his constant sniffles, Harvey didn't bathe very often, always wore thrift-shop clothes, and seemed to be absolutely hopeless at everything. Nobody wanted him. Rejected. Like garbage. I thought of pencil shavings and scrap paper and apple cores.

So grateful, I smiled at Jennifer as her desk touched mine.

"Hey, Jennifer." We both turned. It was Theresa Maxwell, motioning–no, *commanding*–Jennifer to move beside her. I cringed. Everybody else was watching, waiting to see what would happen. Jennifer glanced at me frantically, then looked down and opened her textbook. My heart thumped.

"Pss." That was Richard's harsh whisper. "Jennifer, Theresa's calling you." I felt a knife stab into my chest. "Jennifer. You wanna sit with garbage?"

"Yeah, garbage." I didn't have to turn around to recognize Diane's voice, low and hissing.

"What's going on back there?" shouted Mrs. Kelly. "Come on, hurry up. It doesn't matter who you sit with. Just get busy and practice those verbs."

Jennifer looked past my pleading eyes and clutched the edge of her desk top. No. Please, Jennifer, please don't. But she did. She moved her desk back there, away from me, to sit beside Theresa.

That hurt much worse than being pushed head first into a garbage can.

I looked around desperately. Even Martha Miller was sitting with someone, with Roxanne Campbell. Only Harvey Round was left. "Keri, hurry up," said Mrs. Kelly sternly. "You can work with Harvey."

With burning throat and cloudy wet eyes, I sat beside Harvey and tried to shut out the agony.

When I got on the bus that evening, dragging Dad's grey duffle bag which seemed to weigh a ton by then, Steve slid over and motioned for me to sit beside him. I looked away and sat beside one of the girls from another class.

As the bus started off, I leaned back against the hard plastic seat. Only twenty minutes until I'd get to hug my little Sandy.

Colleen was sitting at the kitchen table drinking a glass of milk with her peanut butter and toast. "How did your talk go?"

"OK."

"Did they like it?"

"How would I know?" I flung the duffle bag on the floor.

"Didn't they say anything about it? What did Miss Phillips say?"

"Nothing much." I turned away.

"How was Steve's talk?"

"Good. I'm going out to ride Sandy."

Colleen followed me to the barn and picked up Pony Bill's halter. I erupted. "How come you always have to do everything with me? Sometimes I just want to be alone." She looked hurt and headed to the house.

All three horses walked towards me, nudging each other.

Then Sandy kicked at Fancy and squealed and grunted. I was amazed to find myself laughing.

It was difficult to tighten the cinch around Sandy's fat barrel, but I managed to do it by myself.

Galloping down the lane on Sandy that afternoon felt like the best thing in the whole world. Her mane flapped in beat to her body motion, and I sat back in the saddle and breathed deeply the rich autumn smells as the ground blurred along beside us.

I turned her and galloped north, past Mom and Dad harvesting in the field. Mom waved from the combine, and Dad winked the headlights of the big grain truck as he drove towards the bins at the edge of the field.

On and on we galloped, Sandy and me, the rhythm and wind healing the pain. The pain of Miss Phillips's scornful eyes and Mr. Fisher's praise and the garbage can and Jennifer sliding her desk away. On and on we galloped. Healing.

Sandy had run almost three kilometres before I realized that she was gasping. I pulled her to a stop and jumped off. Terrified, I stroked her sweat-drenched coat, and felt her heart hammering as her body heaved for air.

Got to walk her, cool her down. She could have had a heart attack. She was so fat, but so willing, she'd never have stopped until I told her to. Or until she died. My skin turned clammy. Thinking about me, only me, working out my pains, I could have destroyed her.

I led her towards home, walking with my arm around her wet neck. After a few minutes her gasping eased to puffing, and at last she started to breathe normally. By the time we reached home, her sweaty coat had almost dried.

Colleen was in the barn, sitting on a bale of straw, patting Matilda. "Steve was here. On his bike. Wanted to talk to you."

"About what?"

"He didn't say. Just asked that you phone him when you get home. He looked sad."

I turned back to Sandy.

"Keri, something happened at school today, didn't it? Something bad. What happened?"

"Nothing much."

I wanted to tell her. I needed to talk to someone. But the pain of wading through all those words and feelings was too much. Mostly, it would be hard to begin. And the longer I left it, the harder it would be.

"Colleen . . ." Now, just spit out the words. Just get started. Colleen would listen. Colleen would care.

"What is it?" she asked softly, waiting.

"Oh, I was just wondering what we're supposed to cook for supper."

Colleen sighed. "Hamburger."

The phone rang after we came back from taking supper out to Mom and Dad in the field. Colleen called up the stairs. "It's Steve."

"Tell him I'm busy doing homework. I don't have time to talk."

A couple of minutes later she trudged up the stairs and knocked at my door. "Listen, Keri, he really wants to talk to you."

"Well, I don't feel like talking to him."

When she came back she said, "Keri, I don't think you should have done that. He sounded really hurt. What on earth happened today?"

"Nothing."

About an hour later I heard a knock on the door. Colleen ran to answer it. She climbed the stairs and opened my door without knocking. "Steve's here. You go down and talk to him right now." I wasn't used to hearing that sternness in her voice.

He was standing beside his bike, twisting his hands around the handle bar. "Keri, I'm really sorry about today. About everything. But especially about them putting you in the garbage can."

"You didn't do anything."

"That's the trouble. I didn't do anything. Because I was scared. You'll never know how much I wanted to do what Ron did. But I was scared and I sat there and did nothing."

Unable to respond, I looked away, the pain still raw like an open wound.

Steve's voice was slow and dejected. "I couldn't be brave riding Fancy because I wasn't scared. But today I was scared to even think of stopping those guys, so I had a chance to be brave. But instead, I proved to myself—and worse, to you—that I am a coward. There were bears under my bed today, and I didn't have the nerve to even go near them."

Oh, how I wished I could just step over and hug him. Stupid tears started to run out of my eyes, so I grabbed Matilda and hid my face in her fur.

I had to say something to let him know I wasn't mad at him. I lifted my face from poor Matilda's wet fur. Why, oh, why did I have to cry so easily? "Steve . . ." But I couldn't get the words out. I choked and tried again. "Steve . . ."

Well, I guess that got the message across, somehow. Because he smiled awkwardly, and said, "Ah, let's go look at the horses."

The horses walked towards us, and Sandy turned her heels to Pony Bill and Fancy, and squealed and grunted like a pig. Steve looked shocked.

"She's not really a pig, she's just jealous," I said, and it felt good to laugh with him.

"When do you have to take her back to Mr. Hanson?"

"Never, I hope. I need her. She's my best friend. If only I could keep her. Mom and Dad have been so busy with harvesting that I haven't had a chance to talk to them again about buying Sandy. But maybe that's good too, because at least they haven't had a chance to tell me to take her back."

The next morning on the bus Steve and Ron were sitting together, and they smiled at me.

Miss Phillips's class was first thing that morning. "In judging your talks, I considered effort, presentation, appropriateness of your exhibits, and so on," she said. "The marks are out of ten. Betty Adams, six. Keri Andersen, two. Darcy Chambers, five. Roxanne Campbell, eight. Len Chan, ten . . ."

Two. Two out of ten. The only others to get that low were Karen and Trevor, and there had been no work at all put into their talks. Even Harvey Round got four out of ten. Richard's torture talk got five. And Gerald with his uncle's talk received eight.

At lunch most of the kids laughingly congratulated Gerald on his mark. "Wow," said Trevor, "I think I'll get *my* uncle to do *my* next talk."

"Better yet," said Sam, smirking and elbowing Trevor, "get *Gerald's* uncle."

Nobody spoke to me at school that day except Steve and Roxanne. Steve stood beside me when I was getting something from my locker. "Keri, how are you doing?" he asked.

"OK."

"About your mark. For the talk. You deserved a lot more. I think you should go talk to Miss Phillips about it. . . ."

"Never. I'd never ever be able to do that." I looked away. "I'm glad that you got eight out of ten. Your talk was really good." I didn't know what else to say, wished I could find the courage to thank him for being friendly to me, for caring.

A few minutes later, I sat on the grass in the shade of a big poplar tree, watching groups of girls saunter out of the school yard, heading downtown as they usually did when the weather was pleasant. They'd always come back flashing new pens and nail polish and lipstick, laughing and bragging as they held their treasures high to show each other.

Of course nobody ever invited me along on their noontime excursions. Mom and Dad wouldn't want me to go downtown at noon, anyway, but how I longed to be invited, at least once.

I opened my book, leaned against the big tree, and started reading.

"Hi, Keri." I looked up, surprised to see Roxanne. She'd hardly said a word to me before.

"What are you reading?" she asked as she sat down on the grass.

"Oh, it's a science fiction book. About some people who get computers implanted in their brains."

She smiled. You didn't see her smile very often. "You read a lot, don't you."

"Yeah. What about you?"

She leaned back on her hands and looked at the sky. "Yeah, I spend a lot of time reading. It's a good way to go into another world."

Her voice made me feel hollow. Roxanne sounded as though she needed to go into another world, often. She seemed desperate for somebody to talk to. But I was afraid, and instead I broke the silence by saying, "It's sure a nice warm day to sit under a tree and read."

She smiled wistfully and asked in a different voice, "What kind of books do you like to read?"

"Oh, anything." The words came out much too flippantly. If only I could summon the courage to start her talking, to let her open up and spill it all out. Why was getting close so scary for me? Why was everything so scary? I felt I would burst with all I wanted to say. Roxanne and I both needed friendship. But I chatted nervously, and felt relieved when the bell rang.

The next few days at recess and noon hour I sat reading under the same tree, half wishing that Roxanne would sit beside me again, half scared that she would. But she didn't.

The best part of each day was coming home to Sandy. Always she seemed so happy to see me, so accepting. Sometimes I saddled her and we ran with the wind, my tense muscles relaxing with her rocking-chair gallop. Sometimes I rode bareback, my legs dangling and swaying as she walked peacefully along the road. Always I talked to her.

Sometimes I wouldn't go for a ride at all. I'd just lie on her soft wide back, my arms around her neck, my face buried in her mane.

Her tiny pointed ears flipped back and forth as I spoke. For the first time in my life I dared talk out loud about anything. At least Sandy would still like me when she really got to know me.

Some days I rode Sandy to visit Mr. Hanson. He would run out to meet us and stroke her, cooing, "My sweet Sandy." I knew he missed her desperately, but I hardly dared think of that.

The days passed. I wore warmer and warmer clothes against the growing sharpness of the air. Farmers' combines crawled from field to field. Soon there would be no more golden swaths to harvest. V's of wild geese honked through the sky. Splendid coloured leaves fell to dusty grass, leaving tree skeletons. Winter was coming, and even worse, Sandy would soon have to be returned.

Chapter 11

The beginning of October brought a new horse for Diane, a magnificent black gelding named King. Of course she had to gallop him into our yard and ask if I'd like to go riding with her. I shrugged my shoulders. "Aw, I'm kinda busy."

Diane smirked.

"He's sixteen point one hands high, even taller than Fancy," Diane said as Mom looked up at King in admiration and stroked his glossy shoulders.

The beginning of October also brought book report time. "I haven't finished reading my book," Jennifer complained one noon while we all sat munching our sandwiches. "How am I going to get a book report done by Thursday?"

"I haven't even started reading a book," said Diane. "I've been so busy riding King. I'll have to find a little book that I can read in two days. I suppose Bookworm Keri has read a dozen books by now."

I tried to laugh with them. Maybe if I could laugh with them, it would smooth things over and they might forget about hating me. It was good they didn't know that I'd read well over a dozen books in September, and was having trouble deciding which one to pick to please Miss Phillips.

"Yeah," said Richard, "Bookworm Keri could write a different book report for each of us."

"I haven't gotten past page five on my book." Trevor sounded boastful. "Some of us are just too busy doing more interesting things than reading books." He looked at me with a mocking pout. "Only trouble is, how do we write our book reports?"

"Just make them up like Gerald," Ron said sarcastically.

"Gerald, you won't!" blurted Natalie. "Aren't you scared Miss Phillips will guess? She's pretty sharp you know."

"Ha. You haven't heard one of my book reports! Ask Jennifer. She'll tell you. Miss Phillips will swallow it hook, line, and sinker."

Theresa looked at him with gooey eyes. "What's it going to be about?"

"You'll see." Gerald held her gaze until she blushed. He loved to unnerve the girls.

When Thursday came, Gerald's book report was stunning. It was about a book called *Go For Broke* by Frances W. Miller. Gerald outlined the plot convincingly. Two boys, enemies at school, had been sent to the nearby stationery store to get art supplies for their teacher. They noticed a brown, mud-covered piece of paper on the sidewalk, and were shocked to discover it to be a one-hundred-dollar bill. Confidently, Gerald told how finding the money affected the relationship between the boys. Turned out, said Gerald, that the hundred-dollar bill had been part of some money stolen from a local convenience store, and together the two boys were able to help solve the crime and, more importantly, came to appreciate and accept each other's strengths and weaknesses.

When he finished, you almost felt like clapping. I glanced at Miss Phillips to see her reaction, but she was writing in her notebook, and it was hard to tell anything.

I had chosen a book about a clumsy, awkward girl's struggle to grow up, and how she eventually becomes a sought-after model, far more interesting and unusual to the world of modelling than the normal type of pretty girl. Kind of an ugly duckling story. But it had been a good book, and I thought it might be the kind of thing that Miss Phillips would appreciate.

I'd put a lot of work into my book report, reading it several times to Sandy in the cozy darkness of the barn. Then I'd even worked on my presentation in front of the mirror in my bedroom, with the desk lamp turned into my face to make things really hard.

But nothing could have dulled the terror I felt when I walked to the front of the room to present my book report. I kept thinking of the horse scat, Miss Phillips's horrified face, the giggling, the garbage can . . .

I stood there, shaking. Then a wonderful thing happened. The words started to flow out of my mouth. All the practising must have helped. By the time I sat down, I was thinking, "Hey, that wasn't so bad." If only Miss Phillips would think so too.

The next day in English class, Miss Phillips read our marks. "They're out of ten," she said. "Betty, six. Keri, eight. Darcy, four . . ."

Eight. I got eight. It was difficult to concentrate on the other students' marks. Eight. Miss Phillips didn't hate me after all.

". . . Richard, three. Diane, four. Gerald, zero . . ."

"Zero? What do you mean zero?" Gerald roared. All heads swivelled to Miss Phillips sitting perfectly straight on the chair at the back of the room.

"Zero. I mean zero," she said sweetly but firmly. "A book report about a book that doesn't exist couldn't be worth anything more."

"What do you mean doesn't exist?" Gerald's face glowed bright red.

"I guess you'd know better than anyone. But what you obviously didn't know is that every library has a set of big books that lists all authors and books in print. All in nice alphabetical order." Miss Phillips looked back at her marks. "Karen, five. Ron, seven." She smiled pleasantly. "Now, everybody, get out your texts, and start reading the poem on page forty-five. We'll discuss the meaning of that poem in a few minutes."

All heads bent to read. The silence was thick as mud.

At recess Gerald exploded. "OK, which one of you slimes told Miss Phillips?"

No one answered. He flung his books in the locker, and glared at us. "Come on. Whoever did it might as well admit it now, because I'm going to make it my business to find out, and then I'll really get you."

Ron said, "Oh, yeah, what would you do, Stevens? Anyway, did it ever occur to you that maybe Phillips figured it out for herself? She's not so dumb, you know."

"You rotten scab, Vander. I bet you're the one. Bet you told Miss Phillips!"

"Wish I had." Ron turned and walked away.

Gerald slammed his locker door. You could almost see steam rising off him as he strode down the hallway in the other direction.

That was Gerald's last made-up book report. But he still continued to copy answers off Roxanne's worksheets in Mr. Fisher's class. And when we had our three days of big tests in the middle of October, he started a cheating operation like I'd never imagined. He wrote facts on slips of paper and hid them in his socks, pockets, pen tops, and pencil case. It worked in Mr. Fisher's social studies test, so he tried it in Mrs. Pratt's science test that afternoon. It was as though Miss Phillips had goaded him; Gerald was determined to prove that he could still outsmart the other teachers.

The next day, in our math test, Trevor put up his hand. "Mr. Korban, my pen's run out of ink. Could I borrow one from Gerald? He's got a few extra."

"Sure," said Mr. Korban, hardly looking when Gerald handed over a pen. As Mr. Korban moved away, I saw Gerald grin at Trevor and then at Sam. My stomach turned to a chunk of ice. They were going to cheat too. Why didn't somebody say something! But I sat quietly and watched as Trevor opened Gerald's pen and took out the piece of paper with math formulas written on it. Mr. Korban was looking the other way too when Trevor pretended to be scratching his back and dropped the paper into Sam's waiting hand.

A few minutes later, Richard adjusted his sock and pulled out another piece of paper. He looked at it in his cupped hand, answered some questions on his paper, then slipped the scrap of paper back to Diane, who later passed it to Jennifer. I couldn't believe what I was seeing. And it went on and on. When had they planned all this? And why, oh, why couldn't Mr. Korban see what they were doing?

At lunch time, Ron said, "Hey, Stevens, you going to use your cheat sheets in Miss Phillips's test this afternoon?"

"Nah, you know facts or formulas aren't much use in Language Arts tests. Anyway, what's it to you? You planning to tell somebody?" Gerald paused, then continued in a low even voice. "Don't bother, Vander. There's twenty-eight of us and only one of you. I wouldn't play those odds if I were you."

For once Ron didn't say anything. He just sat chewing his roast beef sandwich and glared at Gerald. Of course he *wasn't* alone; there were several of us who hadn't been cheating. But how could we dare speak up in front of those other kids?

Before he had even finished his lunch, Ron tramped out of the room. I left a couple of minutes afterward, but he had disappeared. And I didn't get a chance to talk to him later.

When I got home that afternoon, I was shocked to see Mom walking down the lane to meet me, leading Fancy. "Hi, Keri." She was doing her best to speak casually. "We finished harvesting the west field but the last little field by the yard isn't quite dry enough to combine. It'll probably be ready tomorrow afternoon sometime if this good wind keeps blowing.

"Anyway . . ." She patted Fancy and continued in a light voice. "You've been doing so well galloping on Sandy, and it'll soon be time to take her back to Mr. Hanson. You're probably anxious to try again on Fancy, but she's a lot harder to reach to saddle and tighten the cinch, so since I wasn't busy this afternoon, I saddled her up all ready for you to try."

"Oh, Mom, I'm so tired and I have to study for my exams tomorrow. Couldn't I try another day?"

Her voice became stiff and nervous, but still she managed to keep it pleasant. "Keri, please try now. I've got her all ready. Just put your books in the house and change. I'll be waiting for you."

How long can a person take to change her clothes, anyway? Within a few minutes I appeared back in the yard, tense and praying. I tried to put things off by talking. "Where's Dad and Colleen?"

"They went to Rosewood for some groceries. Come on, hurry." She boosted me way up, up onto Fancy, the first time I'd been on her since I'd borrowed Sandy. It must be a kilometre down to the ground, I thought, feeling dizzy.

"She's sure tall."

"Being used to Sandy makes Fancy seem a lot taller to you than she really is."

I walked Fancy around, feeling more uncomfortable than I'd ever felt on her before. Fancy obeyed, but she just wasn't my friend Sandy, and it wasn't right to be up so high.

"Trot her."

"Let me get used to walking her a little more. It's scary up here."

"Keri Marie, why do you have to be scared of everything?"

I trotted Fancy. What a difference between Sandy's jiggly trot and Fancy's powerful earth-eating strides. The ground started to look even further away. Maybe Mom and Dad were right. Getting used to Sandy might have been a bad idea. But how could anything to do with Sandy ever be bad?

"You're doing great," Mom shouted. "Just relax a bit more. Walk her to the lilac bushes and then try cantering back toward me."

I turned Fancy and sat staring at Mom, biting my lip. Come

on, you have to do it, I told myself. You've got to prove that borrowing Sandy was a good idea. Maybe if you canter on Fancy, they'll let you keep Sandy as a friend.

"Hurry up."

I took a deep breath as though I were going to dive under water, kept my eyes focussed on Fancy's ears, and glued one hand around the saddle horn. But as she started to canter, that old familiar terror swelled. My hands did it again, just like before, yanked back on the reins, jerking her to a stop.

"Kick her," Mom yelled. "Keep her going! Don't touch the reins." I thought of Sandy and the pleasure of galloping on her. I must be able to do this. Just get used to the height. I squeezed Fancy's sides again, and again watched my hands pull back.

Mom ran to me, shouting, "What's wrong with you?"

"Please, Mom, I just can't do it." If only I could quit crying. "I'll never ever be able to canter on a tall horse. So what? I can't help it. Please just let me keep Sandy."

"Don't be stupid. You look like an idiot riding that poor little thing with your legs scraping along on the ground. You know Fancy is the right size for you, and she's gentle. This is all in your head. If you hadn't started fooling around with Sandy you'd be having no trouble on Fancy by now."

"But, Mom! Sandy gave me confidence that at least I *can* gallop."

"Some confidence! How come Diane can gallop all over the country on *her* big horse . . ." She broke off then; the words seemed to be choking her. But it wasn't over.

"OK, that does it," she shouted suddenly. "Sandy goes back today. Right now. Get off Fancy, and take Sandy back to Mr. Hanson right now. I'll come and pick you up in an hour in the truck."

Desperately I touched my heels to Fancy. Somehow I kept my hands from pulling those reins, and she started cantering. My eyes focussed on Mom's amazed face, as I sat stiff as ice, too stiff to become part of Fancy's movement. Then

I looked down, and started sliding. I couldn't get my balance on the slippery leather.

So far down to the blurry ground . . .

Chapter 12

I lay on the ice-cold ground, struggling for breath, hurting all over.

Too bad I hadn't died. That would have solved my problems, and Mom and Dad might have missed me enough to forget what a disappointment I'd been. But obviously I had to resign myself to living and to figuring out what to do about myself.

"Keri!" Mom sounded frantic. "Keri, are you OK?"

I lifted my head, but that hurt too much, so I allowed it to flop back.

Mom called again. I opened my eyes and smiled faintly to reassure her that she was stuck with me, for now at least. Gently she pulled me to my feet, her fury gone. I was glad to get up. The ground wasn't too cosy.

Fancy was left on her own while Mom helped me to the house. She fussed over me, her arm around my waist, and that felt good. I was starting to feel better physically too.

Mom made me lie on their bed so I wouldn't have to climb

the stairs. She brought me a glass of water, tucked the quilt around my neck, and fussed over me some more, before she left to unsaddle Fancy.

By the time Dad and Colleen returned, I was feeling much better. I heard them walk into the kitchen. "How did it go?" Dad asked Mom.

"Not so good."

I lay there shocked to realize that the whole thing had been planned.

"What happened?" Dad asked. At least he was concerned.

"She did canter a few steps, but she fell off and really got the breath knocked out of her. She's in our bedroom."

They came in to talk to me, and I tried to act friendly. But I felt betrayed. Why was this so important to them? Some kids never learn to ride in their whole lives, let alone gallop on a big tall horse. And it doesn't matter at all to *their* parents.

What if I'd been cheating in school like the kids in my class today? At least I wasn't doing anything *wrong* by being a chicken. Why couldn't Mom and Dad appreciate me for what I was?

The more I thought about it, the madder I became. By supper time I was fuming.

As Mom passed the bowl of potatoes to me, she remarked, "Well, don't let today's fall scare you too much. At least you did canter a few steps on Fancy. Susan said it even took Diane a while to learn to canter on King. In a day or so you can try again . . ."

I couldn't stand any more. "Oh yeah?" I shouted. "Well I don't care if I never learn. You should be glad that you don't have anything to really worry about. How would you feel if I cheated in school like their precious Diane?" I pushed back my chair, ran up the stairs, slammed my bedroom door, and lay on the bed trembling with anger.

I heard Mom and Dad run up the stairs.

"Leave me alone."

They knocked.

"Go away."

"Keri, let us talk to you," said Mom. "Please."

"Leave me alone."

"Keri, please." That was Dad, really worried.

"Go away. I don't want to talk to you."

Then they did something they'd never done before. They opened my door and walked in without my permission. "Keri," Mom said, "what did you mean about Diane cheating in school?"

"Nothing. I don't want to talk about it."

"Do her parents know?" asked Mom.

"Of course not. And she'd kill me for telling you." I sat up, terrified now. "And don't you dare tell them. Or she'll know for sure who told on her. And she hates me enough already."

"She doesn't hate you."

I moaned and covered my head with my arms. It was amazing how little your parents could know about what went on. But I guess I never told them either.

"When was Diane cheating?" asked Dad.

"I don't want to talk about it. I'm sorry I said it. And don't you guys dare tell her mom and dad."

Mom sighed. "But Keri, they would want to know."

"Then it's up to them to find out."

"No, if it were my daughter, I would want to be told."

"Please, please don't tell them. Anyway, it wasn't just Diane. It was lots of kids. Everybody was doing it." The minute I said that, I knew I shouldn't have. But of course it's as easy to take back spoken words as to catch feathers scattered into the wind.

"What do you mean everybody? Who else was cheating? Does the teacher know? Somebody should be telling the teachers and the kids' parents."

I groaned. Talk about trouble! Desperate, I thought of a way out. "Listen, if I tell you guys all about it, will you promise not to talk to Diane's parents or the teachers or anybody else?"

Mom put her hands on her hips. "No, we certainly won't. Keri, this is something that Susan and Ben must be told." I groaned louder.

Mom started down the stairs. Dad called, "Where are you going?"

"To phone Susan."

Dad was shouting now. "You can't just phone Susan and say, 'Hey, guess what, Diane's cheating.'"

"Why not?"

"You just can't. You'll have to talk to her in person, and bring it up gently and discuss with her what you know about it and everything."

Mom came back up the stairs and sat on my bed.

I lay back against my pillow and wondered what to do next. Boy, I sure can get myself into some messes. I looked out the window. It was getting dark already. But I got the crazy idea that maybe if I went for a ride on Sandy, maybe somehow that would help things.

I slid off my bed and started to pull a sweater over my blouse. "I need to go for a ride on Sandy."

"Are you crazy? We haven't even finished supper." Dad looked tired. "Besides, you've got to study for your last tests tomorrow. And, Keri, we need to get to the bottom of this cheating business."

"I'm not hungry, and I'll be back soon, honestly. I just need to ride for a little while. But please don't phone Diane's parents."

Colleen followed me out the door. I yelled, "I sure don't want you along. You brave, perfect, little turd. How come you never get into any trouble? How come you never have Mom and Dad down your neck?"

To my amazement, she yelled back. "You think you're the only one who's got any problems. You don't know what I think or how I feel about anything! And you don't care either. You don't care about anybody but yourself."

By the time I bridled Sandy and headed down the lane, I felt terrible. Even though I was riding without a saddle, and Sandy's cushioned back was the best couch in the world, my muscles still ached from the fall a couple of hours before. But most of all, my mind ached.

I turned Sandy south and rode for almost half an hour before the hurt began to ebb.

When I returned to the bright lights and warmth of the house, supper was cleared away, and Colleen was wiping the pots and pans. She looked so sad. I wanted desperately to apologize to her, but couldn't find the nerve.

Mom and Dad were sitting in the front room. "Keri," Dad called, "please sit down and talk to us now."

I knew exactly what was coming, so I blurted out, "Diane just cheated once. Today. Please don't tell her parents. I don't think she'll do it again. And the other kids just cheated today too. I don't think they'll do it again either. Please don't talk to the teachers. If the kids get in trouble, they'll hate me even more."

"Nobody hates you. Why do you think people hate you?" asked Mom, her voice softening in disbelief.

I wanted to tell them everything. All about the kids cheating, and how I never seemed able to fit in and how it hurt to be unpopular at school. I wanted to tell them that I hated being a coward, a daughter they could never be proud of. But I didn't dare say a word.

Eventually they let me go study. I didn't sleep very well that night. Friday tomorrow, I thought, staring up at the dark ceiling, Friday and our last tests.

The next morning's French test brought cheating to an entirely new level. Natalie had French conjugations written along her arms, covered by a long-sleeved green sweater. Diane had her own notes written on a piece of paper which she took out of her pen top and held casually under her hand, referring to them every few minutes. Even Peggy Lambert, a preacher's kid, scribbled some answers on a piece of scrap paper, tucked it in her running shoe, and slid her foot forward so Sam could reach down and slip the paper out.

Gerald seemed so proud of his crew. Steve bent over, doing his best to hide his answers from Gerald. But then Steve looked sideways and realized that Theresa was copying from across the aisle. He slid a piece of scrap paper over all except the question he was working on, and tried to cover that one with his cupped hand.

I could hardly believe that Mrs. Kelly didn't see any of this. She was watching, walking around constantly, almost as though she suspected something. But I guess a person can't see everywhere at one time.

Harvey Round sat behind me, and Len and Roxanne on either side, so I didn't have to worry about copiers, but still it was hard to concentrate with all this cheating. I found myself almost glad that it had slipped out to Mom and Dad. Maybe these guys did deserve to get into trouble. But it would be me in trouble, because Diane would know who had told.

With all the guilt and tension and wondering, I didn't get my French exam finished. At noon I sat under my favourite tree and read. After two weeks of cold wet weather, a few days of pure blue sky and brilliant sunshine seemed wondrous. Even though October nights were always cold in Alberta, October days could sometimes be as warm as summer. We called it Indian Summer.

When I got home from school, Mom and Dad were harvesting that last field. I saw Dad by the bins across the lane, unloading wheat. As he drove away to get another load of grain from the combine's hopper, he winked the truck's headlights at me, and I waved.

Colleen was in the barn, combing Pony Bill's tail. She didn't look at me when I walked in.

I went to get Sandy. As usual she squealed and grunted to keep Fancy away from me. I tried to pat Fancy anyway, maybe because I felt guilty for ignoring her so much, but Sandy was determined not to share my affections, and Fancy gave up and walked away with her head hanging. For the first time I felt sorry for that big horse. But it was flattering to think that Sandy liked me so much.

I put the tiny halter on Sandy and led her into the barn. "Sure is a nice warm day," I said to Colleen.

"Sure is," she answered quietly. I looked at her, and she looked away quickly, but I'd seen them. Tears.

I tied up Sandy and sat on a straw bale. "Colleen, I'm sorry."

"It's OK," she started, her voice flat. The next moment she was crying, big sobs shaking her body. "You don't like me and nobody at school likes me either, and you don't even know or care."

"What do you mean, nobody at school likes you? Everybody likes you."

"No they don't. And I don't know why. I try really hard to make them like me, but they don't. And sometimes, even if they seem to, it's just for a while. Sometimes I feel so lonely I think I'll die."

I could hardly believe what I was hearing. Confident Colleen, sobbing as though she would break, crying about awful loneliness. It was impossible. I picked up Matilda and hugged her, and then handed her to Colleen who sat down on the bale beside me.

"Gee, Col, I'm really sorry. And I'd like to be your friend, except I don't think sisters are supposed to be friends." And then we were laughing through our tears. Purring like an old washing machine, Matilda arched her back and turned tiny circles between us. "You should see your face," said Colleen, giggling.

I laughed. "Yours too." We had smeared the tears with our dirty hands.

"Those filthy horses," said Colleen, holding out her blackened hands and laughing harder.

"I know what, Col. It's such a nice day. Let's give the horses a bath."

Despite the warmth of the air, the horses stamped and snorted, protesting against the icy water from the hose. We shampooed them, used cream rinse to make their manes and tails tangle-free, then stepped back to admire our handiwork. They looked gorgeous, drying in the sun, the long, late-afternoon rays glinting gold on their soft clean coats.

"We should take a picture of them," Colleen said. "I'm sure Mom won't mind if we use her camera."

“Only one thing,” I said. “Sandy’s tail still doesn’t look clean.”

“It’s just stained. A white tail always looks stained from manure.”

“Not in horse shows on TV and circuses and things. The white horses have pure white tails. Maybe they bleach them. I want Sandy to look perfect for the picture. Let’s try bleaching her tail.”

Colleen looked uncertain, but I ran to the house to get the bleach.

Chapter 13

"How strong should we make the bleach solution?" asked Colleen.

"Let's read the directions." I looked at the label. "Laundry. No, we don't want that. Kitchen and bathroom cleaning. No, not that either. Ah, here it is. Stain removal. For stubborn stains . . ."

Colleen smiled. "Yeah, I guess that's what you'd call this."

"Right. For stubborn stains, soak item . . ." We both laughed. ". . . soak *item* for 5 minutes in a solution of 125 ml bleach per 5 litres of hot sudsy water, followed by regular washing with bleach and detergent."

I ran back to the house, filled an old plastic pail with hot water, squirted in some detergent, then carried it out to the barn, sloshing with every stride.

"Did you bring the measuring cup for the bleach?" asked Colleen.

"We can guess."

"No, I think we'd better get it. I'll run back to the house."

But I had already screwed the cap off the bottle, and was pouring bleach into the water. "There, that should be about right."

"Sure looked like more than one-twenty-five millilitres to me," Colleen said, not too pleased.

"Don't worry, it'll just do the job better." I bunched up Sandy's tail and stuffed it into the pail. I felt so excited, thinking of how white and beautiful her long full tail would look on the picture. If I had to give Sandy back, at least I would have a perfect photo of her. Maybe I could get a huge enlargement made, like a poster, to hang on my wall forever.

"Keri, are you timing five minutes?"

"I can't see my watch when I'm holding the pail up like this. Here, you hold it."

That little horse stood so patiently, even when Colleen got tired and leaned both her arms and the pail hard against Sandy's fat rump.

"OK. That's about five minutes."

Colleen happily set the pail down. But then her face froze. "Oh no!" I followed her gaze to Sandy's very soapy tail. It was yellow. Yellow, not white. Almost orange-yellow.

The yellow didn't rinse out, not with cold water, not with hot water, not even with hot water and soap, nor with hot water and detergent.

A white pony with a bright yellow tail. What would Mr. Hanson say?

By now the sun was threatening to disappear, chilling the air, and I had abandoned all ideas of taking a picture. But we had to get this yellow off her tail somehow.

"Shampoo," I said, feeling an uncomfortable knot between my ribs. "Maybe that would work better than plain soap or detergent."

"Keri, it's getting late. We've got to go in and make supper."

"What if you start supper and I get the shampoo and try one more time before Mom and Dad get done? If they see this yellow tail tomorrow morning they're going to kill me."

"It'll be dark soon, and Sandy might catch pneumonia in the cold night air if you get her all wet again now."

"I'll rub her tail and her rump dry with a towel when I'm done."

"OK." Colleen untied Pony Bill to lead him out to the pasture. "Oh, he's so clean. What a pity to let him out now when he's still damp. He'll just roll in their old dirt hole and get all filthy again."

Sandy whinnied unhappily as Pony Bill was led away. She figured a couple of hours was long enough to stand patiently, and didn't see why she had to stay tied when he could go free.

I walked with Colleen to the house. Into the bucket full of clean warm water I squirted almost half the bottle of shampoo, then took a towel with me out to the barn. Sandy whinnied when she heard me coming.

"Don't worry, Sweet Sandy, you'll soon get to go free."

Even with the shampoo, Sandy's tail stubbornly remained brilliant yellow.

I rinsed her again, and sighed. I rubbed with the towel, but couldn't get her tail or rump dried. The rest of her coat was still a bit damp too.

How I hated the idea of turning Sandy out to the pasture, knowing that she'd immediately roll in the dirt. After all our work. She looked so incredibly white—except for her yellow tail. If she rolled now, the dirt would turn to mud and really stick to her damp coat, and she'd look much worse than she did before her bath.

I could leave her tied up in the barn until after supper. By then she'd be dry and much less likely to roll. Even if she did roll when she was dry, the dirt wouldn't stick to her coat.

It was getting dark. Soon I had to go to the house. Yes, that's what I'd do—leave Sandy tied for a while. But as I walked away, she whinnied plaintively. To desert her now would break her heart.

I turned back, untied her, and was going to lead her into the pasture. But then I thought, why not let her graze on the lawn until after supper? She'd be dry in a couple of hours and then I could put her back into the pasture.

I led Sandy to the back lawn so she'd have company. Pony Bill and Fancy whinnied and trotted to the fence to touch Sandy's nose across the barbed wire. She grunted and squealed, and I smiled. Sandy loved the company of those two horses, missed them desperately when they weren't with her, but always had to show them she was boss.

Within a few minutes, Sandy started munching grass, and Pony Bill and Fancy lowered their heads to the coarser pasture grass across the fence. I left Sandy's halter on, with the lead rope dragging on the lawn behind her, but she just turned her head slightly as she grazed so she didn't step on the rope.

Everything looked so peaceful and calm. It was dark enough now so that the yellow in Sandy's tail didn't show, and she looked silvery and magic in the soft glow of the fading sunset. I watched her for a few more minutes, almost as though I were tied there. When I saw the twinkle of the first star I made my wish, then sighed and walked reluctantly into the bright lights of the house to help Colleen with supper.

We had almost finished frying the sausages when the phone rang.

I answered it. "Hello?"

"Keri Marie Andersen," the voice whispered, "I am going to kill you."

"Diane . . ."

My heart pounded, my throat went tight, and my saliva turned to glue.

"How dare you make up a lie about me cheating in a test at school!" Diane hissed.

"Lie?" I was aghast. "What do you mean lie? Of course you were cheating–yesterday and today in all the tests."

"Yeah? Well, that's your word against mine, isn't it?" The sarcasm was as thick as the hatred in her voice. "Seems your mom was over this morning and she had a nice little story to tell my mom, courtesy of Keri Andersen."

Her tone sharpened. "You just wait until we're all finished with you at school. You thought it was bad to be put in a garbage can? When we're done, you'll wish it was just that!"

The phone crashed down, and I stood for a second listening to the dial tone.

"What's wrong, Keri?"

I put the receiver back and made my sticky mouth form words. "Mom went to talk to Mrs. Spalding this morning. Diane's ready to kill me. She's going to tell the other kids at school, and they'll really be out to get me." I bit my lip to hold back tears. "Col, what am I going to do?"

"Boy, I don't know." Colleen looked worried too.

Just then we heard the grain truck drive into the yard, and within a couple of minutes Mom and Dad walked into the house.

"It didn't take you long to get me into trouble, did it?" I shouted as soon as Mom was in the door.

Mom looked defensive. "Susan was glad I'd told her. She really thanked me."

"Well, I can tell you Diane isn't thanking me."

"She will someday. Something like this has to be stopped sooner or later, and the sooner the better."

"Can't you see how much I'll be hated because of this? Nobody likes an informer. Diane's ready to kill me. And worse yet, she's telling her parents that I made it all up."

"What do you mean 'made it all up'?" asked Dad.

"Lying. She says I'm lying. That she didn't cheat." My mind was racing, scrambling for a way out of this. "Hey, what if we did say that I was lying, that Diane didn't really cheat. Then she wouldn't be in trouble with her parents, so she wouldn't hate me as much and I wouldn't be in trouble with the kids at school . . ." The words tumbled out, sounding better all the time.

"Are you crazy?" Mom shouted. "That's the dumbest thing I've ever heard."

"Keri," said Dad, "Diane needs to learn that cheating is not a good thing to do."

"Why do I have to get killed in the process?"

Mom put her hand on my shoulder. "You're over-dramatizing this. Don't worry, in a day or so it'll all blow over. Diane will realize that she was in the wrong . . ."

I pushed her arm away. "You sure don't know Diane! Oh, why did I have to blurt out about her cheating? Me and my big mouth. I should have my tongue ripped out."

Just then the phone rang. Dad answered it. "Sure, Susan. We're just going to start eating supper. About half an hour from now would be fine." He listened then for a minute or so, looking more and more serious. "Well . . . we'd better wait and talk about it all when you get here. See you in about half an hour."

He put down the phone. "They want to come over and talk with us. You're right, Keri, when they confronted Diane, she denied the whole thing. Said you made it all up. And it almost sounded as though they might believe her. They're coming with Diane to get to the bottom of it."

I moaned, I pleaded, but Mom and Dad refused to even consider my idea about pretending that I had been lying.

We forced down our supper, hardly talking, and then hurried through the dishes. I was sweeping the floor when the Spalding's car lights swung into the yard.

In walked a very tense mother and father and their sullen, irate daughter. We sat in the living room, all except Colleen who was sitting at the kitchen table with a book. But of course we all knew that she would be listening too.

Ben broke the awkward silence. "I guess we might as well get right to the point. Diane insists that Keri made up this story to get her in trouble because she's jealous of Diane and doesn't like her."

My eyes opened wide. Jealous! I almost leaped from the couch, but Dad put his arm on my lap. "Ben, we've never known Keri to lie."

Diane's mom gulped. Her voice sounded cold and heavy. "I assure you that we've never known Diane to lie either."

Mom's voice was even colder. "Well! So you think our daughter is the one who is lying."

"You can take it however you want," said Diane's mom, her hands trembling, her eyes flashing. This was getting worse and worse. What if their age-old friendship got wrecked all because of me and my big mouth?

I desperately wanted to shout, Diane's right, I lied! I lied!

Frozen silence filled the next few seconds until Dad said quietly, "Listen, Susan, you and Elaine have been friends for so many years. Please don't let anything spoil that. And please just give me a couple of minutes to tell you what we know about this situation. Then we'll listen to whatever you want to say about it. But, please, let's discuss this as adults – and friends."

Ben leaned forward. Almost as if in slow motion, his Adam's apple moved up and then down. "Go ahead, Ed. We'll listen."

Dad took a deep breath and then told the whole terrible story about me falling off Fancy and being so angry at them, and how mom had just mentioned about Diane cantering on her big horse, and how I had blurted out that at least I didn't cheat like Diane.

Then he paused and looked around. "Keri clammed up right after that. She wouldn't tell us anything more about the cheating. She begged us not to tell you. When you phoned tonight, she kept begging us to say that she did lie, so Diane wouldn't be in trouble and wouldn't hate her."

He swallowed. My dad didn't usually talk a lot, so this was starting to tell on him. "I'm not saying that Keri would never lie. When I was a kid, I lied sometimes, and I remember my parents being convinced that I was telling the truth. But the way that Keri has acted about this whole thing just doesn't seem to me to be the way she'd act if she was trying to get Diane into trouble by lying."

Diane's mom started to speak, but Dad said, "One more thing. If either Keri or Colleen ever gets accused of cheating or something like that, we'd want to know too. Good kids sometimes get into bad circumstances and need guidance. And that's the only reason that Elaine went to talk to you about this. Please believe us."

Susan looked at Diane, then looked back to Mom. "Elaine, I'm sorry." Then her voice stiffened. "Now, Diane, please tell us what happened in your tests at school. And we want the truth."

Diane stared at the rug. "The other kids were doing it, so I tried too. I got some answers from slips of paper that the other kids passed to me. But I never did it before."

"And you'll never do it again," her father said, embarrassed and furious. "Ed and Elaine, I'm really sorry about all this. I think we'd better take Diane home and figure out what to do about her."

"Ben, please don't be too hard on her," Dad said. "Kids make mistakes. They learn from their mistakes. I really don't think she'll do it again."

"Please don't go yet," said Mom. "Stay and have a cup of coffee."

Ben looked sad. "Thanks, but I think we'd better get home."

They headed towards the door. But even after they got their coats on, they talked a while longer. Diane's mom put her arm around my mom's waist, and they leaned their heads against each other's shoulders like they've always done, and I felt a lump in my throat, hoping I could find a close friend like that some day. Obviously it wasn't going to be Diane. Her jaw muscles clenched, and I had no trouble lip-reading the message she snarled: "Wait till Monday."

Before they left, Mrs. Spalding put her arm around my shoulder and squeezed me. That felt good, except that it made Diane glare as though she would like to knife me.

As soon as they left I went to bed. I couldn't bear to talk to anybody any more about anything. I went to bed, but couldn't sleep. Thick dread clamped my chest like a vise. An informer, a traitor, that's how Gerald and the other cheaters were going to think of me. This would be a lot worse than getting praise from Mr. Fisher or bringing horse manure to school. Diane was right. When she and the other kids got through with me, I'd be wishing I were in a garbage pail.

Then I heard it, soft footsteps coming up the stairs. Mom. She knocked at the door and spoke gently, with a catch in her voice that I had never heard before. "Keri, please, could I talk to you?"

She walked in slowly and sat on my bed, twisting her hands, looking down at the floor, and she didn't speak for a couple of minutes. I had never seen Mom at a loss for words, and it made me feel very uneasy, like standing on paper-thin ice over a deep lake.

"Keri, sometimes we don't . . . sometimes parents don't . . . appreciate what we have." She looked up, then turned her head away. "And maybe pushing somebody to do something that isn't really important – like cantering on some old horse – well, maybe it means we haven't appreciated that person . . . as . . . as they really are."

I felt as though my heart had stopped. Could Mom be saying what I thought she was saying?

She was silent again. Then it seemed as though she was talking to herself. "But maybe we push because we care too much." She looked up with an awful sadness. "Or maybe it's because we haven't cared enough. Oh, I don't know. I don't know."

She sighed. "Keri, some things matter . . . and some things don't. And maybe sometimes I forget which is which. A mother should be kinda proud of any daughter who had the courage not to be involved in cheating."

Her voice became stronger. "Things like that are important. And lots of other things. Like how hard that daughter works at school and around the farm. And how that girl needs to be cared about because growing up isn't very easy . . ."

She reached out and stroked my hand, oh so gently, then quickly stood up and headed out of the room. I lay in bed, unable to call her back. Just before she closed the door, she said, "I don't blame you if you give up on me sometimes."

I lay there, staring at the closed door. A strange confusion and yet a strange peace grew within me. Mixed in with all that was dread about Monday. Tomorrow was Saturday. Two more days before the vultures could get at me. But at least I would be coming home to people who did care. And maybe it wasn't so easy to be a parent either. Monday. Two more days from now.

I woke several times that night with the sheets wound around my neck and upper body, my feet naked and cold. Each time, I got up, tucked the stupid sheets in, then lay twisting from side to side, until sleep would claim me again.

Finally I woke to sunshine. I got up and looked out the window. A layer of white sparkling crystals covered everything. It had frozen very hard last night. Strange how much worse that made me feel. I put my housecoat over my pyjamas and padded down the stairs in my bare feet.

Mom and Colleen were eating their cereal. They greeted me warmly and I was amazed at how glad I felt to see them. I was standing at the counter, reaching for a bowl when Dad flung the door open. He stood as though paralyzed, his face white, white as . . .

"Sandy. . ." he cried. "Sandy! She's dead!"

Chapter 14

"Dead? Sandy dead?" Mom whispered, while the vise tightened around my chest and my legs turned to rubber.

"Somehow she got out of the pasture . . ." Dad's hands were shaking. The vise threatened to cut me in two. How could I have forgotten Sandy out on the lawn last night?

"Somehow she got out. She got into the grain bin that I was filling last night. She must have been eating wheat all night. And now she's dead."

Colleen and Mom started howling and ran with Dad out to the yard. I followed, my legs so numb I couldn't feel them move. This was only a nightmare, it just had to be.

Dad led us across the lane and over to the open wheat bin where the white swollen pony lay on churned-up dirt with her legs in the air. Was that my voice that screamed? Mom and Colleen stood crying.

Sandy! You have to be alive.

Maybe she's sick. Or maybe even just sleeping. I bent to hug her, but that short white neck was stiff and that beautiful fine head was heavy, impossible to lift. And I had never known her soft thick coat to feel so cold, icy cold.

I sat on the ground, watching her, commanding myself to wake from this nightmare, to find myself back in my warm comfortable bed. Then I could get dressed and sneak out to the lawn behind the house to hug Sandy and lead her into the pasture. No one would ever know that I'd forgotten her out overnight, and I would be able to ride her as soon as the sun melted the white frost covering the crisp brown grass.

Dad touched my foot. His hand seemed hot, very hot. I looked down at my bare feet, almost blue on the frozen grass.

"Keri, you have to get some slippers or boots on," he said gently.

I couldn't answer, couldn't move. A few minutes later, or maybe it was a few seconds or a few hours, Colleen ran back from the house with my pink slippers with the fluffy lining, and, crying, slipped them on my feet. I hadn't even known that she had been gone, and I couldn't feel the fluffiness of the slippers against my toes. She wrapped my old grey jacket around my shoulders, covering my pink-flowered housecoat.

I stood up, not daring to touch that unyielding cold white body again, but powerless to leave. Mom had her arm around me, her head against my head.

"I can't figure out how it turned her tail yellow," said Dad, and Colleen wailed louder.

If only I could cry. My throat burned as though with acid, and my lungs could hardly pull air against the agony, but the tears would not come. Even words wouldn't come. Finally Dad took my arm and led me away, but the pain dragged along behind me like Sandy's halter rope had dragged behind her the night before. But I couldn't turn my head to avoid stepping on it.

They sat me at the breakfast table. In a trance I chewed on toast and jam that had no taste at all. Colleen cried and then Mom started crying again, and Dad left the house with his shoulders hunched over.

By the time he returned, Colleen and Mom had finished

the breakfast dishes, but I was still sitting at the table. "I can't figure it out," said Dad sadly. "I've walked all around the edge of the horse pasture, and there's no break in the wire. Both gates are shut. I just can't understand how she got out."

Staring at the jam drops on my plate, I held my hands knotted over the back of my head, my elbows leaning on toast crumbs. "I left her out." Those were the first words I'd managed to speak, and it seemed as though a stranger had said them.

Dad's voice ignited. "You left her out?"

The three of them stared with wide red eyes.

"Yes. I left her out on the lawn last night." My voice sounded so flat and empty, but I pushed the words out because I had to. "We bathed the horses. And her tail got yellow. From the bleach. I tried to wash out the yellow. And I left her on the lawn. To graze until after supper. So she could dry off. But I didn't remember her. Because Diane and her mom and dad came."

Dad groaned and sat down with his hand over his eyes. Mom cried out, "Keri, how could you?" Colleen sobbed, big gasping sobs.

I climbed the stairs to my room and changed my clothes, as mechanical as a robot. When I passed through the kitchen again, Colleen was sitting at the table, crying as though she would choke. Dad had his arm around her, his face against her hair. Mom was leaning at the counter, staring blindly out through the window. No one said a thing as I walked past them and out the door.

Mr. Hanson. I had to talk to Mr. Hanson.

I didn't want to ride my bike to his place. I didn't want to ride anything but Sandy, and now I'd never ride her again. Not ever. It didn't matter that the walk to Mr. Hanson's would be three kilometres. What mattered was that I'd have to go past the Lomar place; their house was so close to the road. I couldn't bear to run into Steve right now.

A blue jay squawked and swooped from the sunflowers in the garden as I started down the lane. The sun's gold had already melted the white frost crystals, and the world sparkled with diamonds in the grass. But a sharp knife turned harder into my chest, and I walked faster and faster in time to its jabs.

Steve was in his front yard raking leaves. He smiled, waved, and called. I lifted my hand in a pale greeting, but couldn't force my wooden lips into a smile, couldn't call hi even though that's all it would have taken to allow me to walk on alone to Mr. Hanson's without having to stop and talk. I made my feet walk faster. Maybe Steve would realize that I didn't want him to come running after me.

It didn't work. He ran out of the yard. "Hey, Keri, wait up a minute."

I kept walking, my legs reaching along the gravel road, each step bringing me closer and closer to Mr. Hanson's place. Oh, Mr. Hanson, what are you going to say to me? What are you going to do to me? But you're the one I need to talk to, because you're the one who loved Sandy like I did.

"Keri, Keri," Steve called again, running, catching up to me. "Is something wrong? Why won't you stop?"

I had no way out. I kept walking, but he pulled the words from me, about Sandy and why I'd forgotten her out last night, about Diane and her parents and the cheating. He gasped as he listened, put his hand on my arm, and walked with me. "Oh, Keri. I'm so sorry." He brushed his hand awkwardly across his eyes, and still I couldn't cry. Me, Keri Andersen, the cry-baby who hadn't been able to hold back tears because of a garbage can or a tall living horse . . .

We walked briskly, silently, Steve's warm hand still on my arm, until we were almost halfway to Mr. Hanson's place. "Do you want me to come with you to talk to Mr. Hanson?" he asked gently.

"No. I have to do this alone."

"OK." He took his hand off my arm and touched my cheek. He started to say something, but then he turned to walk slowly back home, his head bent low. I stood watching him, wishing I could yell out thanks, but somehow I knew that wouldn't be enough, so I turned and pressed on, even more quickly than before.

I was almost running by the time Mr. Hanson saw me.

He came to meet me, shouting from his lane, "Hi Keri, where's my Sweet Sandy?"

But then he got a look at my face, and it seemed as though he knew right away, without me having to say anything. "Oh, Keri."

"She's dead. Mr. Hanson, you trusted me to take care of her, and now she's dead. And it's my fault. I loved her so much, more than anything in the whole world." Mr. Hanson reached his huge calloused hands to enfold me. And then I cried. My tears washed over his faded plaid shirt as we sat on a big rock and cried together, cried for yesterday and today and for all the tomorrows that would come without our Sandy.

He let me blow my nose on his big worn polka-dot cloth handkerchief before he used it. When all the crying had drained us empty, we sat quietly on the big rock by the gate, listening to the chickadees in his caragana hedge.

There was something that I had to talk about. After a few minutes more of sunshine and silence, I forced myself to start. "Mr. Hanson?"

"Yes, Keri?"

"I don't know how to say this, but, well, I need to ask you, but, uh, I'm the one who borrowed Sandy and it's my fault that she's dead, and I will pay you for her. But I can just pay some of it right now, twenty-seven dollars, because that's all I have in the bank from birthday money and other things, and as I get more, well, I'll pay you as I get it, and it will take a long time, but I don't want to ask Mom and Dad for any of it because it was all my fault. Besides, they didn't want me to borrow her, but I'm glad I did because at least I got to know her, but of course I'm not really glad because then she wouldn't be dead. But I *will* pay for her, Mr. Hanson, really I will, every bit of what she would have cost. I'll pay it as I get the money even though it will take me a few years."

Mr. Hanson listened, blowing his nose again in the wet handkerchief. He put his vein-corded hand on my knee. "Keri, have you got any money with you?"

Puzzled, I reached into both jacket pockets to dig out the contents and display them on my open hands. On my right palm were some dirty oats, a red elastic band, a hoof pick, a ball point pen, one quarter, three dimes, two pennies, and a crumpled yellow flyer from a Moreland theatre advertising October's movies.

On my other hand lay some more oats and dirt, a grubby stuck-together Kleenex, two quarters, two dimes, one nickel, six pennies, and a fence staple.

"Good," said Mr. Hanson, picking out the coins. "Seventy-five. Eighty. Ninety. One dollar. One thirty. One, two, three, four, five, six, seven, eight." He looked up. "One dollar and thirty-eight cents. Now, let's see if I can find me a piece of paper." He fished around in his pockets but could only find some nails and other odds and ends.

"It's all right," he said, "we'll use this," and he took the yellow movie flyer from my hand. He smoothed out the paper, took the ball point pen and tried it on the back of the flyer. The pen wouldn't write. He laid the flyer on the rock and scratched big circles to start the ink. Finally the ink began to mark, faintly at first, but then bold and blotty. "Good enough."

He held his tongue out the side of his mouth to help him concentrate. "R.R. 1, Rosewood, Alberta. What's the date today?"

"October sixteenth," I answered, afraid to see what he would write next.

"October fourteenth," he wrote with the blotty pen. "Sold to Keri Andersen, one white pony mare named Sandy for the sum of $1.38. PAID IN FULL. Signed Mr. Peder Hanson."

He folded the dirty yellow flyer and laid it on my hand along with the ball point pen. Then he slid my coins into his shirt pocket. "There, I guess that about takes care of it."

"But Mr. Hanson," I cried, "I can't pay for Sandy with just one dollar and thirty-eight cents."

"There wasn't enough money in the whole world to pay for her. So I guess one dollar and thirty-eight cents is as good an amount as any other amount a person could name."

"But Mr. Hanson . . ."

"Paid in full means paid in full. So I don't think we can discuss that any more." He blew his nose again into the soggy handkerchief. And I wiped mine on the dirty stuck-together Kleenex I'd found in my pocket.

"Keri, let's go to the house. I was up real early this morning and made some bread. Guess I must have known we'd need it. It just came out of the oven. And we can have some butter and some good peach jam on it. And a glass of milk."

He took my hand and led me to the house, where the first thing he did was get each of us a clean dry handkerchief.

It was late afternoon before I started my long walk back, dreading to return home, dreading the rest of the weekend. Only last night Diane's promise of revenge had seemed like the biggest, most terrible thing in the world. Now, that all seemed to be a far-away threat, as unbelievable as the horror movie advertised on the flyer.

When I got home, Mom had made me an angel food cake. It seemed to have no taste at all, but how velvet and soft it felt in my mouth.

I wandered around the yard. Fancy and Pony Bill whinnied and ran to meet me. Fancy hung her head over the fence, begging to be patted. "Go away. I don't want you!" She pulled back frightened, but again reached her head over the fence, her ears flicking forward and backward, looking puzzled but eager. "Go away. I don't want you. Not ever."

"She can't help that Sandy died, and she can't help that she's tall," said a dreary voice. I spun around to see Colleen, her eyes wet and swollen.

"Well, I don't want her, and I don't ever want any horse again."

Colleen's mouth quivered. "Just remember, you're not the only one who's hurting. I loved Sandy too."

She walked away, but within a couple of minutes returned and put Matilda into my arms. "Thanks, Col." She didn't answer, just stood stroking Fancy. Matilda purred and snuggled up against my face.

"Keri, you pat Matilda. Why can't you pat Fancy? It wouldn't hurt you to show her a little love. She hasn't done you any wrong."

"You don't understand anything," I said.

Somehow I lived through that endless weekend of lonely nothing. When you've had a tooth pulled, your tongue keeps finding the hole.

On Monday morning when I climbed onto the bus, Steve slid over for me, and I sat beside him, the first time ever. Jennifer turned around, her face twisted in disgust. "Keri Andersen, you narc. Diane phoned to tell about you ratting on us. And she phoned all the others too. You're going to be sorry."

"Hey," Steve said, "Keri didn't mean to tell. It just slipped out because her parents were giving her a bad time comparing her to Diane . . ."

Jennifer smirked. "How come you're sticking up for Keri? You must be in love with her, eh? Poor you."

He turned red and looked out the window. Just then the bus stopped at Diane's place.

Chapter 15

"Hey, hey, what do we have here?" hooted Diane, as she settled in beside Jennifer and turned to stare at Steve and me. "Steve, what's a nice guy like you doing with a rat like her?"

Steve's eyes flared. "You just don't know her, that's all."

"Oh? I've known Keri a lot longer than you have, *Stevie.* That's the trouble. I really know what she's like. When you get to know her, you won't like her either. Nobody does. Just ask Jennifer."

"Yeah, she used to be my best friend," Jennifer sneered. "Some friend."

I winced. No use hoping any more that Jennifer still cared about me, even a little.

None of us talked again until we got to school. Gerald and his pack scowled and jeered as I walked into the classroom. "You narc. You rat."

Someone had written with chalk on my desk, in big letters, "LOOK INSIDE." I sat down and saw a folded piece of lined paper. How I hated to open it. But I knew they were watching to see what I'd do. The paper shook in my hands as I unfolded it and read, "Why don't you eat some rat poison for lunch."

Without looking around, I crumpled the paper and shoved it back into my desk just as Mr. Korban walked in to take attendance.

First class was language arts. I could hardly concentrate on anything Miss Phillips was saying, even when she read our exam marks and mine was one of the highest. I kept staring out the window, wishing I could be lying on Sandy's back, talking to her, even just one more time.

At recess I noticed Gerald, Trevor, and Richard striding down the hallway towards me. Before I could swerve or run, they grabbed me and carried me towards the boys' bathroom. Only one shriek escaped before Gerald clamped his hand around my mouth. I kicked Richard in the ribs but he just growled and grabbed my legs harder so I couldn't even move them. I scratched Gerald on the face. "You fight like a rat too!" he muttered, really angry then, and wrenched my arm behind my back.

They pushed me into the bathroom. The door swung closed and I twisted around. The bathroom was full, guys sitting on the sinks, standing at the smelly urinals, all staring at me. I stared back at them, horrified, and it was obvious that they weren't too thrilled either.

I yanked the door open. Richard, Gerald, and Trevor stood blocking my escape, their arms folded, their faces leering. Frantically I fought them, but they shoved me back into the bathroom.

Again the door swung shut and again I yanked it open. But this time they were gone! I rushed into the hall and crashed straight into Mr. Korban.

"Keri, what on earth?"

Oh, if only the floor could open up and swallow me. I looked around desperately and saw Richard and the other two disappearing quickly down the hallway.

"Mr. Korban, it was an accident. Sorry. So sorry," I mumbled, and then started running.

"Keri, Keri," called Mr. Korban, but I kept running, and made it out into the school yard, and leaned against a tree, panting and trembling.

Mr. Korban. He'd never think the same of me again. How could I ever explain to him what had happened?

Our very next class was math. How could I possibly face Mr. Korban? But it would be even worse if I didn't show up for class.

I went into the room just as the bell rang. When Mr. Korban walked in he looked at me, but I avoided his puzzled gaze, and he started the math lesson. Several times during the period, I noticed Mr. Korban watching me, but he never made a comment. I stared out the window. The naked trees swayed as the wind strengthened, swirling dust and dried brown leaves across the road. The sky changed from grey to white, and then snow started to fall. Snow, big swirling snowflakes, our first snowfall. White like Sandy, cold as death.

I had just started eating my lunch when Diane walked in and sneered, "I don't know if we should be eating with a rat in our room."

"Maybe we should exterminate her," said Richard, and several of the others laughed harshly.

"Hey, why don't you guys leave Keri alone?" Steve's voice sounded dry and tense. All heads swivelled to look at him. Steve didn't usually talk much but when he did, people listened. "She didn't mean to tell about the cheating; it just slipped out because her parents were bugging her and comparing her to Diane."

You could almost cut the silence with a knife. Then Richard snorted, "How come you're sticking up for her, Lomar? She ain't worth sticking up for."

Trevor and Gerald laughed, but Steve struggled on. "Don't you guys have any feelings? Give Keri a break. She's had a really rough weekend."

"Oh, yeah? How rough?" Gerald challenged.

Steve looked startled. "Well, uh, her pony died and . . ."

"How'd it die?" Richard cut in. "I bet she killed it."

"No. No!" He was almost shouting now. "It was an accident. Keri was so scared and worried after telling about the cheating that she forgot and left her pony out . . ." Oh, no, I thought. Steve, please don't tell them. It'll just make things worse. But he kept talking, trying desperately to make them understand. ". . . and the pony got into grain and ate all night and died . . ."

"Ha!" yelled Diane. "So you *did* kill the pony, Keri. Boy, you're really something. It's not bad enough to be a traitor, you've got to be a murderer too."

"Maybe we'll have to hang her," Richard said, the words so smooth and cold that my neck prickled.

Steve looked frantic. "Listen, I told you guys about the pony because I thought then maybe you'd understand how awful Keri must be feeling and maybe leave her alone . . . " They howled with laughter. Steve stared down at his desk and said nothing more.

I felt so badly for him. I wanted to tell him how much I appreciated how he'd stuck up for me, but he finished his lunch quickly and then disappeared into the hallway.

Ron stood beside me when I was getting my jacket from my locker. "Sorry to hear about the pony." He touched my hand with his pen. "Hey, Keri, don't let them other kids get to you. You're OK, you know."

I went for a walk. The raw wind knifed my face and froze my tears, stabbing through my jacket as though it were made of tissue paper. The streets were almost empty. The kids who usually wandered downtown in packs at noon hour had stayed in the classrooms and hallways, hiding from the wind and snow.

By the time I got back to the school the ground was white, and it was time for the bell to ring.

That afternoon, after recess, Mr. Fisher had the social studies exam marks ready for us. As soon as we filed in, he began to lecture the class about how poorly the majority of them had done in the exam. Then he paused, rocked on his feet, puffed up his chest, and announced, "I'm so proud of Keri. You should all congratulate her. She got one hundred percent."

Gerald hissed under his breath. Diane and Jennifer turned around and sneered. Sam narrowed his eyes and screwed up his face contemptuously. "Yes, it's wonderful to have a student like Keri," continued Mr. Fisher, completely oblivious to what was happening. "Now if all of you would try to be more like her . . ."

Gerald hissed again and Richard stuck his finger in his mouth, pretending that he was throwing up. It was just too much. I ran for the door, shouting at Mr. Fisher, "I hate you, I hate you!"

"What on earth?" Mr. Fisher called as I pulled open the door. "Oh, dear. Could one of you girls please go find out what's happened?" His voice carried after me as I ran down the hallway.

In the security of a locked bathroom cubicle, I sat fully clothed on the toilet seat, my throat burning, my hands shaking.

"Keri." It was Roxanne. "Keri, please let me talk to you."

"Go away. Please."

"No. Mr. Fisher sent me to get you."

"Well, I'm not going back to his class." We were hardly talking above a whisper, but our voices echoed strangely in the empty bathroom. I didn't sound like myself.

"You have to go back," Roxanne said, "or Mr. Fisher might report you to the principal. And then you'll be in trouble."

"I don't care."

"Well, I do. Keri, I'm really sorry about your pony." She hesitated. "And I wish I had dared to tell on them all for cheating. I'm just too much of a coward, that's all."

It was weird talking through a bathroom door like that, instead of face to face. It wasn't nearly as scary as looking into someone's eyes. "Roxanne, I don't know what to do. I just wish I could die."

"I know how you feel. Honest. Sometimes I feel that way too. But a person has to keep going somehow. Maybe tomorrow will be better. Just keep believing that. It really does seem to help. And someday, things might be a whole lot better." She sighed. "At least that's what my Aunt Agnes tells me, and she's my favourite person in the whole world, even though I hardly ever get to see her any more."

Roxanne needed to talk. I could feel it. Even through the bathroom door, I could sense that there was a lot more to this girl than what I saw in class.

So listen, I told myself. Reach out to her. Maybe it would help if she could tell somebody. Roxanne had cared about me, and now was my chance to care about her.

But when I opened the cubicle door my nerve vanished. I walked to one of the sinks, braced my arms on it, and put my head down. "Thanks," I mumbled. "I guess we'd better get back to Mr. Fisher's class." That's all I managed to say. I couldn't find the courage to take on *her* pain too. Surely I already had enough to think about, enough to cry about, without sharing somebody else's problems.

Mr. Fisher was waiting in the hall to meet us when we emerged from the bathroom.

"Mr. Fisher . . ." I gulped. "I'm sorry."

"What on earth happened? Who do you hate? Who were you talking to? What's going on?"

It was hard to believe that he hadn't realized I'd been shouting at him. But I sure wasn't going to tell him. "Mr. Fisher, I'm really sorry, I won't let it happen again. Please forgive me."

He beamed, rocking on his heels. "My dear girl, there's nothing to forgive. You're such a wonderful student. If you just tell me, I'll deal with the guilty party who was upsetting you, believe me. I'll see that it never happens again."

"Oh, it's OK." I looked at Roxanne and then back to Mr. Fisher. "I . . . I think I've got it straightened out, Mr. Fisher. But thanks very much."

In the crowded hallway on the way to French class, Steve walked beside me. "Keri, I'm so sorry that I told them about

Sandy. I didn't mean to, but it just came out. I made things so much worse . . ."

"No, you made things better just by sticking up for me."

"Better? It was horrible what they said to you after I told them about Sandy."

"Steve, I feel so awful about Sandy, and so lonely for her that I could die. What Diane and Richard said is the truth, and I deserve it. Anyhow, they would have found out sooner or later." He still looked so sad and ashamed. "Steve, you dared to stick up for me in front of all of them. Talk about bears under the bed! There's nothing imaginary about how mean those guys can be. I really appreciate how you tried."

"You mean it? You're not mad at me?"

"Mad at you? Oh, Steve, I was wondering how I could ever thank you!"

His ears turned pink and he seemed to struggle before he said, "Oh, just send a cheque." Then he bowed, a silly, deep dramatic bow. "A couple of thousand dollars for services rendered." For the first time in four days I actually found myself laughing. And he smiled, a warm, reaching smile that needed no more words.

Funny how a smile can warm a whole day, even a day as horrible and hostile as mine had been. The memory of that smile still kept glowing when Mrs. Kelly read our French marks and I'd almost failed because I hadn't been able to concentrate enough to even finish the exam.

When I got home, Colleen was out talking to Pony Bill. Big powdery snowflakes were drifting and swirling like lost ashes. Fancy came over to the fence. Her back and neck were covered with snowflakes, and there were even a few caught on her eyelashes.

Remembering Steve's smile, I reached out to pat Fancy. And a snowflake landed on the back of my hand.

Chapter 16

The strangest thing happened the next morning at school. No one acted horrible to me. Diane and Jennifer said hi. Even Gerald, Richard, Sam, and Trevor said hi. Karen and Natalie stopped to talk to me. "It's sure too bad about your little pony," said Karen, patting a stray hair in place beside her ear.

"That's for sure." Natalie looked at me awkwardly. "You must feel awful."

"Yeah, I do. Thanks." What was going on here?

The pressure had stopped so abruptly that it was like stepping from a hurricane into a warm kitchen. I asked Steve if he'd talked to any of them again, but he hadn't, and he'd been watching, puzzled too by their complete change of behaviour. Could it be possible that Ron or maybe even Len had said something to them that could have worked such magic? I didn't dare ask.

At noon, Karen and Natalie talked to me again, small friendly ordinary talk that I'd always craved to be included in. They were such popular girls. Why would they be talking to me like this at anytime, least of all after what had happened in the last few days?

After a few minutes of chatting, Natalie said, "I wonder who will be running for secretary."

Everyone had been surprised the day before when the announcement boomed over the intercom that there had to be a new election for the position of secretary on the students' council. Tricia Moraine, from Mrs. Kelly's homeroom, was the present secretary. She was a beautiful, popular girl, and had seemed so at ease standing up at assembly reporting on student council activities. But Tricia had to quit now because her dad had just been transferred to Edmonton and they were moving in a week.

"Somebody from our room should try to run," Karen said.

"Yeah, for sure." Natalie looked at me. "Keri, why don't you try? We could nominate you and help with your campaign."

"Me. Are you crazy? Not me!" I was flabbergasted, flattered, and terrified by the idea. "Definitely not me. Why not you, Natalie? Or Karen? Either of you! Or Diane or Jennifer?" Someone popular, I wanted to say, but was afraid to.

"Aw, you've got to be really good at writing reports and all that to be secretary. You know Karen and I would be hopeless at it. We can't even write a decent book report. And Diane and Jennifer are worse. We wouldn't stand a chance. But you're a brain at language arts just like Tricia. If we nominated you and helped make posters and really got out and campaigned, who knows, maybe you could win."

"Yeah, Keri, I bet you could win." Karen sounded excited. "It would sure be an honour for somebody from our room to be elected to a position on student council."

My brain said whoa, there's something very wrong here, don't be ridiculous. But my heart said great, here's your chance at last, your chance to be included, to be somebody.

Anyway, within a few minutes they had me talked into it. They discussed it with the rest of the class, and before the bell rang, it was agreed that I would be nominated for secretary of the students' council of our school.

My heart thumped as I walked down the hall to our next class, surrounded by the popular girls all talking to me and making plans for my campaign. Even Diane seemed excited, waving her purple fingernails around her purple sweater and purple earrings, chatting about posters and the cheers we could make for noon in the hallways. Theresa put her arm around my shoulders, and giggled about something. I could smell her very expensive perfume.

All of it was so strange, so unreal. It was like a wave that lifted me up and carried me along.

On the bus Jennifer saved a seat for me, and Diane sat beside Linda Evans, right behind us. Linda told us that no one in her class was running for the position of secretary, so she'd try to persuade her whole class to vote for me. As we chatted, I noticed Steve and Ron at the back of the bus, watching us intently.

How good it felt to burst into the kitchen with such unbelievable news and to see the joy it brought to Mom and Dad. Now if only there could be Sandy to tell the good news to. I'd lie on her back and hug her and smile and she'd be so relieved that for once I wasn't sad about something.

I was feeding the chickens when I saw Steve walking through the snow into our yard. I ran to meet him, delighted. But he answered my greeting in a guarded serious tone. "Keri, I need to talk to you."

"What's wrong?"

"I wish I knew." He spoke slowly. "I don't like it, Keri. Something's up. Why are they being so nice to you at school all of a sudden?"

"Because they want me to run for secretary."

He shook his head. "But *why* do they want you to run?"

I glared at him. "Because they want somebody from our room to win, and the person has to be good at writing reports and all that. You know Diane and Natalie and all the other popular girls aren't."

Steve clenched his fist and thumped it against his leg. "But Roxanne is good at writing, and so is Peggy. Why you? There's something more to this than we know."

"What do you mean, why me? Thanks a lot. I thought you'd be happy for me." I gulped, fighting back tears. "Besides, Roxanne's always such a loner and so sad and dreary. Why should they choose her?" I gulped, feeling terrible for having said that. "And . . . and Peggy wouldn't be interested in it anyway, I bet. You should be glad that they want me."

"But, Keri, yesterday they were awful to you. Why would they change overnight? And even if it is just because of the student council thing, can't you see that they're just using you?"

"Well, let them use me, then." I stamped my foot. "For the first time in my life I've got lots of friends . . ."

"Friends!" He snorted. "I hardly call them friends."

"Steve, I think you're jealous."

"Jealous?" He laughed, a high-pitched sarcastic laugh. "Jealous?"

"Yeah, they're paying more attention to me than to you." I realized that I was shouting.

He flinched as though I had slapped him. Then he shook his head. "Keri, Keri. Can't you see that there must be something else going on? And whatever it is, I don't like it. And neither does Ron. We were talking about it on the bus, and we can't figure it out."

I bit my lip and turned away from him. "Well, I don't see what there is to figure out, and I don't see why you and Ron can't just be happy for me."

He left soon afterwards. I pushed the snow off a bale of straw by the chicken coop and sat down to pat Matilda, my mind confused, my stomach churning. What I needed right now was to go for a gallop on my Sandy.

Fancy. I could ride *her.* I wandered out to the pasture. She trotted to meet me, whinnying, sliding to a stop in the snow. But I looked up, way up at her, and decided not to bother.

She followed me back to the barn. I gave her a handful of oats and patted her. She touched her velvet nose to my cheek. Why, oh why, couldn't Fancy have died instead of Sandy, I wondered, and then I hated myself for even thinking it.

I reached up and scratched her face. "Poor Fancy!"

At noon the next day, Natalie and Theresa asked if I wanted to go with them downtown. How could I say no? Surely Mom and Dad would forgive me just this once. After all, they wanted me to have friends, and that meant I'd have to fit in. "Sure." I tried to sound casual so they wouldn't know how grateful I was.

As we crunched through the snow, I realized that I didn't have any money with me. And they always brought back little things from their downtown jaunts. Well, it wouldn't hurt if I didn't buy anything, but I might as well tell them from the start. Somehow I found the nerve to say, "I don't have any money with me today."

They giggled strangely and nudged each other. "No problem," said Natalie. And they giggled again.

I blushed, wishing I hadn't mentioned it. They had to be laughing because of how poor I was compared to them. For years Colleen and I had begged Mom and Dad, but we had never managed to convince them that we needed an allowance. There never was much extra money floating around on our farm, and this year the swaths had been rained on several times, so it would be low-quality grain and bring a low price. This definitely wouldn't be a good year to dredge up the subject of an allowance.

Natalie interrupted my thoughts. "I think I'll get some lipstick and nail polish to match this colour," she said, referring to her soft new pink angora mitts, hat, and scarf. "Keri, how come you never wear any make-up or anything?"

"Oh, I don't know."

"Would you like us to get some for you?" asked Natalie.

"Naw, it's OK."

"No problem," said Theresa, and they laughed again. "And don't worry about paying me back."

It was the weirdest shopping trip. The girls dragged me all over the store to see one thing or another, but we always seemed to be leaving somebody behind.

"Keri, you have to see these colours," Natalie said, pulling me over to the lipstick counter. I had to leave Theresa by the pens. Then, "Keri, what do you think of this blouse?" Theresa was in the clothing area now and I had to trudge over there, leaving Natalie at the make-up. The clerk kept offering me assistance, but what could I say? "Just browsing, thanks."

By the end, I was tired and bored, and felt like a ping-pong ball. I was so glad when both girls sauntered to the door, and Natalie said, "Well, I don't see anything I want today. Maybe we should head back to school."

We'd gone a couple of blocks when Natalie looked over her shoulder and then pulled a new tube of lipstick and a bottle of nailpolish out of her jacket pocket. She held them up to her scarf, and asked coyly, "Well, what do you think of the colour match?"

My mouth opened, but no words would come out. From her coat sleeve, Theresa pulled a lime green fluorescent pen, and held it up proudly. "Keri, how do you like my new pen?"

I gulped. "Uh, it's pretty."

"Check your pockets." Natalie smiled. "You never know what you might find." I tried to hide my growing terror as I reached in my pocket, and sure enough, there was a tube of lipstick.

"Nice, eh?" asked Natalie proudly. "I thought that colour would look good on you."

"Uh, yeah, it's real nice." I hoped they wouldn't see my hand trembling. I wanted to drop it, or hand it to Natalie, but didn't dare, so I shoved it back into my pocket. The metal tube felt red hot in my hand.

I wanted to run back to school and bury myself in a book and pretend this hadn't happened. It didn't make any sense.

There probably wasn't a richer kid in the whole school than Natalie, and Theresa was a famous accountant's daughter. They each had their own phone and TV and VCR in their bedrooms, and their allowances were legendary. And here they were stealing lipstick and pens from a store. It didn't make any sense at all.

My heart pounded to think that I was included in this too. I had visions of Mom and Dad visiting their daughter in jail. For sure Mom wouldn't be making my favourite cake to bring along.

What to do? I didn't dare tell anyone. Just look at the trouble I'd put myself in because I let it slip about Diane's cheating.

I watched Karen and Peggy when they came back from downtown a few minutes after us, showing off a rainbow key ring and a fancy pen. Only that morning, I would have assumed that they had bought those things.

I couldn't talk to Steve about all this, but I wondered if he suspected. Did any of the guys go downtown to do their noon shoplifting too? My stomach ached thinking of it all.

"Keri, aren't you going to try your new lipstick?" asked Natalie.

"Yeah, come on," Theresa pressed. "Let's see how it looks on you."

If ever I wished for courage it was then. But Peggy and Karen joined in the clamour, and finally I went into the bathroom with them, broke the package seal, and applied the stolen lipstick to my trembling lips. Pale pink. "Looks great," said Karen, and they all agreed.

Walking down the lane on the way home, I rubbed off the lipstick, but some pink must still have been left, because both Mom and Dad seemed to give me a double take, although they made no comment.

They asked about my campaigning. "There's nothing to tell you yet. Nominations won't be approved until tomorrow afternoon, so we're not allowed to start campaigning until then."

Mom put her arm around me. "We're so excited for you. And don't worry, even if you don't win, we'll be just as proud." She gave me a little squeeze that reminded me of Friday night when she had come to my bedroom to talk. It seemed like a hundred years ago.

Before I went to bed, Colleen remarked, "Make sure you don't get lipstick on your pillow." I made a face at her. But in the bathroom, I used soap to rub off every trace before I could look at myself in the mirror.

It took a long time for me to fall asleep that night. I heard Mom and Dad shut off the TV news and get ready for bed. Still I rooted around under the covers, trying to relax.

When I did drift off, I dreamed of bathing Sandy. In the dream I couldn't get her clean; in fact each time I washed her, she got dirtier and dirtier. I awoke raw with pain and lay listening to the fridge hum, hearing a coyote howl, and a calf moo once in a while.

What would I say if the girls asked me to go downtown with them the next day? Why was I so scared of what people thought of me? Why couldn't I just be me? Why couldn't I find the courage to stand up to what I believed? But at least this way, I didn't have to worry about being treated horribly by the other kids at school. If I could just play their game, go along with them, this would all work out somehow.

As soon as I arrived at school, Theresa asked, "How come you're not wearing your lipstick? You look so much better with some colour." They pressured me until I went into the bathroom and took the tube out of my pocket.

"Let me try." Natalie took the lipstick from me, and with great concentration drew my lips in pink, and stood back smiling to admire her artistry. Then she took some of her own mascara and applied that to my blinking eyelashes.

When I walked into class, Steve stared at me but didn't smile.

At noon Natalie asked, "Keri, are you coming downtown with us?"

"Oh, I don't know. Maybe you guys should go ahead."

"Aw, come on." Karen frowned. "What's wrong?"

"Nothing. I just thought maybe I'd stay at school. I have a few things I wanted to do . . ."

"Don't you want to come with us?" asked Natalie. "You seemed happy to go with us yesterday."

Theresa's eyes narrowed. "Don't forget about the nice pink lipstick you're wearing."

"Come on, Keri." Natalie looked uneasy. "I wanted to invite you to my sleep-over party next week. You can help us plan it while we're walking downtown."

Theresa stared as though she were looking right through me. "And on our way downtown, we can do some more planning for your election campaign too . . ."

Yes, I needed them now. I'd sure look stupid in front of the whole school running for the position with nobody backing me.

"Aw, Keri, come with us," Natalie urged.

"Sure." I heard my voice, thin and shaky. "What are we waiting for?"

The sun shone golden, melting that first snow, claiming a bit more Indian Summer before winter could set in permanently. Normally, such a day would cheer me tremendously. But trudging along with Karen, Natalie, and Theresa through the slush in my new running shoes, my heart ached and my feet were cold and wet. I hadn't dared to wear my boots. I knew these girls wore running shoes even through rain or blizzards.

There's a lot more to this being popular than meets the eye, I thought, feeling frightened and out-of-control. When you're totally unpopular, you're pretty well free to do what you want at recess and lunch time, whether it's to read a book or just sit feeling lonely. Nobody asks you to do anything, so you don't have to figure out how to say no.

When you're with the popular crowd, you pretty much

have to do what everybody else wants, talk about what they think is interesting. As we walked downtown, our feet getting wetter and wetter, I found myself wishing I knew more about the different rock groups, the latest songs, and all the other things that the girls were chatting about.

Most of all, I kept dreading what was to happen in the store. More bears, I thought. They seemed to be everywhere.

What if we got caught? I tried to persuade myself not to worry. They'd obviously done this dozens of times and had never been caught. Maybe it wasn't as dangerous as I thought. Or maybe they did usually pay for all the things. Maybe yesterday was the first time, and they wouldn't be doing it again. Maybe they just shoplifted yesterday to show off to me.

Into a store we went. The clerk hovered over us. Surely she could hear my heart thudding. The girls browsed, sometimes separately, sometimes together, chatting, exclaiming, and laughing. They looked so relaxed.

I was relieved when Natalie said, "I think I'll buy this magazine, and then we can go." She paid for it, and our little herd left the store. But before we got back to the school, Natalie pulled a packaged nail file from her pocket. Not to be outdone, Karen showed off a new lipstick and a ballpoint pen.

Theresa extracted a cute little dog-shaped eraser from her jeans pocket. "What did you get, Keri?"

"Uh, nothing."

"Why not?" Her voice was sharp, accusing.

Natalie put her arm around my shoulders. "Aw, Keri's just got a lot to get used to. You're all right, aren't you, Keri?"

The next day we spent the noon hour in our classroom, making posters. Even Gerald, Trevor, Richard, and Sam made some posters. So did Diane and Jennifer. I watched them, amazed. Steve and Ron helped too, but they seemed so serious; they didn't laugh and joke with the other kids.

So that I would know the popular songs, I had listened to the radio all the evening before, while doing my homework. It made the homework a lot harder, and I really didn't like some of the songs at all, but at least I was beginning to feel a bit more like one of the gang. I was working on my poster, talking happily about the latest hit songs, when I glanced up and saw Steve watching me sadly. I bent my head quickly and made thick firm letters with the red felt pen. I was starting to get angry. Who did he think he was, making me feel rotten every time he looked at me?

That afternoon the announcement came over the intercom that three girls would be running for the position of secretary of the student council: Marlene Durham, Keri Andersen, and Nancy Flannigan. It seemed impossible to have my name listed with two of the most gorgeous, sought-after girls in our school.

What if the really impossible happened and I actually won? I thought of how terrifying it would be to stand up in Tricia's old spot and have to deliver a report in front of the whole school. My throat tightened. I'd better stop this before it got out of hand. Got out of hand? It was already out of hand.

There would be one thing even worse than winning. What if nobody voted for me? Absolutely nobody. I looked around at my classmates. Well, at least I'd have their votes. And Linda's classmates . . .

"Campaigning must be finished by Thursday morning at recess. In the first period after lunch, the school will assemble in the auditorium for five-minute speeches by the candidates. Voting will be in the classrooms immediately after the speeches. Results will be announced by three-thirty that afternoon."

Chapter 17

Monday morning in language arts class, I happened to turn around and caught Diane looking at me with a smirk which she instantly rearranged into a thick, wide smile.

A few times that week when we were putting up posters or giving our campaign cheers in the hallways, I caught some of the kids from other classes smirking at me and then turning away as soon as I met their eyes. Whenever it happened, I felt tight and terrified. I didn't know what it meant and I wasn't sure that I wanted to.

Many times, surrounded by Theresa and Natalie's group, I noticed Roxanne watching me, her lips drawn into a thin, worried line. I felt a flash of anger each time because it reminded me of the way Steve and Ron had been looking at me lately. I felt like shouting at them all, "Why can't you just leave me alone?"

Even if I had wanted to talk to Roxanne now, I would have hardly dared to, because Theresa always made fun of her behind her back. Theresa could be vicious if she thought you were a bore, like Roxanne, or a weirdo, like Harvey. So it was best for me to try to fit in as perfectly as possible.

Things seemed so smooth at home that week. Even Dad hadn't mentioned anything again about riding Fancy, and I wondered if it was because he was proud I was running for student council, or because he felt sorry for me about Sandy's death.

Mom and Dad were busy that week of my campaigning, trying to get the fields cultivated before winter set in. They took turns driving the tractor, giving each other a few hours rest. It would soon be time to wean the calves. We usually weaned them about the end of October. I was dreading it. Colleen and I would have to ride our horses to help separate the frantic calves from their determined mothers.

In the past few months, whenever we worked the cattle, Colleen and I always had the job of chasing and sorting them on horseback while Mom and Dad worked on foot. They opened and closed gates, branded, castrated, or vaccinated, depending on what had to be done. Fancy had discovered that she didn't have to work very aggressively with me on board, and everybody usually ended up mad at me for letting the cattle slip by.

The night before the election, I was lying on my back, staring at my upside-down pictures of horses and the new ones of rock groups, with my radio blaring out the latest hit songs, thinking about calf weaning and school campaigning. How different my life had been this week, and how much different it would be if I did win!

Colleen knocked at the door, came in, and sat on my bed. I turned the radio down. She didn't have much to say, yet seemed reluctant to leave. "Keri, you've hardly talked to me this past week."

"What do you want to talk about?"

"I don't know. Anything."

After a few more moments of awkward silence, she left, and I turned the radio volume up and tried to concentrate on my homework.

The next morning passed in a blur. At noon we weren't allowed to campaign anyway, so Karen, Natalie, and Theresa asked if I wanted to go downtown with them. I had been determined to say no this time, and to stick by it, but still I gave in and went along, hating myself.

The sun shone brightly. All of our first snowfall had melted days before, leaving dry brown grass along dusty sidewalks.

Theresa led us into the E. M. Variety Store. The girls wandered around, calling to me and to each other, discussing and handling various items, moving apart, working different areas of the store. I felt the same vise tighten around my chest again. How, oh, how could I get the nerve to remove myself from this situation, and to never get into it again?

The clerk tried to be everywhere at once, watching us closely. But when the phone rang, she moved to answer it, and Theresa pushed her arm against my side. "Come on, let's go look at some shoes," she said, and moved away from the lipstick counter towards Natalie.

There was something strange about the way Theresa had pushed against me, a kind of double movement. I reached into the left pocket of my blue jacket. My cold fingers closed around something. Another tube of lipstick. Frantically I looked around. Natalie and Theresa were inspecting a pair of running shoes, and glancing sideways at the clerk who was listening to the phone with a serious, puzzled expression. I cupped my hand around the lipstick package, eased it out of my pocket onto the counter beside the others, then stood as though paralysed, my heart hammering.

I glanced back at the clerk just as she riveted her eyes on me, put down the phone, and started for me. I looked to the other girls, but could hardly believe what was happening. They were walking calmly but quickly toward the door.

"Excuse me," said the clerk with an iron voice, "could you let me see what's in your pockets?"

Surely my heart would slam right through my jacket. The clerk thrust her hands into both my pockets, while I realized with horror that I hadn't checked my right one. What if they'd put something in there too? The clerk must have heard my sigh of relief when her hands came out of both pockets with nothing but a couple of old Kleenexes. Natalie, Karen, and Theresa were almost out the door.

"What? Nothing?" the clerk cried. The three girls spun around, shocked. Their shock turned to horror as they realized that I had seen their expressions plainly. Then they vanished through the door, leaving me with the embarrassed clerk.

"I, uh. Well, uh, I'm sorry," she said, very puzzled.

I had to tread carefully, or I could end up looking guilty. "Did this have anything to do with your phone call?"

Her eyes narrowed in confusion. "Well, yes." Then she became suspicious. "What do you know about that phone call?"

I couldn't help but laugh. Comic relief, I guess you'd call it, but I laughed until the tears came. The clerk didn't understand. "Look, if you think this is a joke, I can call the police," she said angrily. "In fact, that's what I should have done in the first place. I know you had something in your pocket. You were the only one with a blue jacket."

Yes, it fit together. "Somebody phoned you and said that there was a girl in your store with a blue jacket and that she was shoplifting, and to check her pockets. Right?"

She stepped back. "How did you know? What's going on here anyway? Is this some kind of trick?"

"It sure is. I'm afraid somebody was trying to play a trick, but it wasn't on you. It was on me. Honestly, I haven't stolen anything. You can check my pockets again, and my sleeves, anywhere . . ."

"Just get out of here." She put her hands on her hips. "And don't come back into this store ever again. Get going."

"Thanks so much." I was so relieved by my close escape that I couldn't quit smiling.

"Wipe that stupid grin off your face. You young people today think you're so smart. I'm sorry we even have to serve you."

My thoughts swarmed as I walked back to school alone. The whole thing had obviously been planned, down to the last detail. It was no coincidence that Theresa had slipped the lipstick into my pocket, just as the clerk was distracted by the tip-off phone call. But who had been on the other end of the line? Who had planned to get me arrested for shoplifting? Diane? Gerald? One of the other students in my class?

It was too horrible to imagine the disgrace of being caught shoplifting. My family would die. And imagine the disgrace in front of the whole school of being arrested the day I was up for election.

And that was the crazy part. Theresa, Natalie, and Karen had been my main campaign managers. Why would they want to bring disgrace upon themselves by having their candidate arrested the day of the election? No one could ever be in any kind of trouble and hold a position on student council. If I won the election, the principal would have to take the position away from me and call another vote. That would certainly bring humiliation and disgrace on our whole class for nominating and supporting such a candidate.

Supporting. My mind froze.

Supporting. Yes, they'd made posters and called out cheers in the hallways when I was around. But how many times had I caught them looking at me oddly, and what about those strange smirks from kids in other classes?

Yes, finally everything made sense.

I raced into the school. Knowing what was to have happened made me shiver. I could imagine the whole school listening breathlessly while the election results came over the intercom: Marlene and Nancy each getting hundreds of votes and me getting none.

The principal's secretary wasn't in any hurry. "Hi, Keri. Are you ready for your big speech? I guess you'll hardly be able to wait for three-thirty this afternoon."

"Please, Mrs. Waldron, may I talk to Mr. Gilbert right away? It's really important."

Mr. Gilbert looked up as I walked into his office. "Hello, Keri. I bet you're getting excited about the election."

"Mr. Gilbert, I want to withdraw my name."

He gulped. "What do you mean?"

"I don't want to run."

"Why not?" He frowned.

"Please believe me, I just can't run. And I can't say why. Trust me that it's important."

"But in a few minutes the whole school is going to assemble to hear your speeches, and the ballots are all printed up and ready to distribute to each classroom . . ."

"Mr. Gilbert, you could just announce before the speeches start that Keri Andersen has withdrawn. Everybody can cross my name off their ballot as they vote. I'm really sorry about all this, but I just can't run."

He sighed. "Keri, what's wrong?"

"I wish I could tell you about it, Mr. Gilbert. But I can't. Please forgive me."

I hurried into the auditorium on legs of rubber.

Steve and Ron. There they were, talking together as they chose their seats. I needed to be with them. Maybe some of their strength would help buoy me up through this. But would they want me sitting beside them after the way I'd been treating them the last week?

"Hi," I said shakily. "Would you guys let me sit with you?"

"Friend or foe, they're all welcome," said Ron. "We're not smart enough to know the difference."

I laughed nervously and sat beside them.

Mr. Gilbert walked onto the stage, and the ruckus settled to loud whispering. He raised his hand. "Quiet, please. Before the candidates speak, I have an important announcement to make. Keri Andersen has withdrawn her nomination."

Complete silence. Then came a mounting tide of gasps and giggles and wide-eyed stares from all over the auditorium. So many of the students were now directing their smirks at Diane, Natalie, Karen, and Theresa, who sat sullen and red-faced, staring down at the metal chair legs in front of them.

Steve and Ron stared at me, bewildered, but obviously relieved.

As we filed out of the auditorium, Ron tapped me on the shoulder. "Well, kid, I sure don't understand what's going on, but somehow I have the funny feeling that you came out a winner."

At recess I told them the whole story. They thought it was a great joke, but promised not to say a thing to Diane or anyone else about what had happened. I figured Diane was probably embarrassed enough already, and I sure didn't want to push her into trying any more tricks.

When Diane stepped onto the school bus, she didn't look at anyone.

Jennifer sat beside Diane, but she glanced at me once with a hint of a smile, as though she had found the whole thing a bit of a joke too.

I sat behind Steve and Ron. "What you gonna tell your old man and old lady?" asked Ron.

"Got any suggestions?"

"Well, better not tell them the whole crazy story or they'll be telling Diane's parents, and here we go again . . ." He grimaced and chopped at his neck with the side of his hand. "Maybe you could say you withdrew for personal reasons. Then you and Diane would be about even in score."

Colleen ran down the lane to meet me. Before she got a chance to ask, I said, "Colleen, I withdrew my name. I didn't run for secretary."

Strange, I'd expected her to be disappointed. But she smiled openly and said, "Good. You might have won and then you'd be thinking you're too great."

Instead of getting mad, I started to laugh, a good deep cleansing laugh. Colleen chuckled as she kicked a stone down the lane. Then despite my resolve to tell no one else about the shoplifting and the phone call and the trick Diane had planned, it all came tumbling out.

Colleen's eyes widened. "Wow! So Diane and those others must have gone around behind your back, telling all the kids in the school not to vote for you. They must have said that they were getting even because of the cheating thing. But just imagine them keeping all this secret, and still campaigning and everything." She shook her head ruefully. "Wow. And I guess they wanted to get you in trouble for shoplifting today just to really put you down."

She looked up. "Or maybe they were worried that the kids in other classes might feel sorry for you and vote for you anyway. Yeah. So they'd get you caught shoplifting. That way you'd get the position ripped away even if you did win. Either way, they couldn't lose. Or so they figured."

"Gee, I never thought of that angle. But I bet you're right."

Then Colleen looked very serious. "What are you going to tell Mom and Dad?"

"I don't know. What do you think?"

"Tell them that you decided not to run because it was too scary. In fact that's not really a lie. It sure would have been scary to get no votes. Yeah, tell them you decided at the last minute that it was too scary. They'd believe that."

"Oh, thanks a lot. Do you want them to think I'm even more of a coward than they already do?" My temper flared like fire on dry grass. "Thanks a lot. Just because you're such a brave little fart."

"Hey, don't yell at me. It's not my fault I'm the way I am. You asked me for an excuse to give Mom and Dad. I gave you one. Take it or leave it."

I ended up taking it. It was the easiest way out. But I winced at their disappointment.

On Saturday morning when Dad said, "Do you guys feel like weaning the calves today?" I answered, "You bet."

It went easier than I expected it to. After almost getting arrested for shoplifting, and after the near-disaster of the election, farm work of any kind seemed so normal. The cows still churned and shoved, their calves darting frantically around Fancy to stay glued to their moms. My legs still got scraped and squished against slivery wooden corral panels, and most of all, Fancy was still uncomfortably tall compared with Sandy. But I did it.

Even when Wanda came charging at me, I turned Fancy straight into her side as I kicked my boot at her face. For once I found myself glad to be mounted on such a tall horse. Wicked Wanda spun away and ran bellowing into the holding corral. "Good for you, Keri!" yelled Dad, beaming. I looked at Mom and Colleen. They grinned.

I lay in bed that night listening to the bawling of separated moms and babies, and thinking. No one ever got much sleep the first couple of nights after weaning. It would take a few days before the bawling died down as they gradually got used to being separated. Maybe I could gradually get used to things too, like Fancy's height. Then I'd be able to gallop on her. And maybe I'd be able to do other things too. Harder things.

I had handled Fancy in the corral full of milling cattle, and even braved Wanda. And somehow, I had managed to outwit Diane with her carefully-laid plan to humiliate me through the election. Surely that was about the worst she'd be able to come up with. And if not, I guess I'd just have to face whatever she thought of next.

Maybe this was kind of a new beginning. Nothing wrong with being scared of things, just as long as you still try. That's what Steve had said. I drifted off to sleep, feeling good.

On Monday morning, after Mr. Korban marked attendance, he announced that our class and Mr. Ross's homeroom class would be going on a day-long ski trip to Lake Louise on November 28. That was less than one month away. A ski trip.

Absolutely thrilled, most of the kids in our class spent the noon hour talking about the trip. Diane said, "I took two years of ski lessons from a Canadian national champion when we lived in Toronto. I can show you guys some of the things he taught me."

I was less than thrilled; my resolve from the night before had completely melted. The idea of skiing had always sent shivers along my spine. Talk about heights. If Fancy seemed high, what about a mountain? I'd be sure to fall and break my neck on the way down.

Mr. Korban handed out information and permission sheets to take home. Maybe I could just tear up the sheets and say nothing about it. No, that wouldn't work, because Diane's mom would be sure to talk about the ski trip with my mom. Mr. Korban clinched it. "You have to return these sheets by Friday, signed by your parents saying whether or not they want you to go. If they check yes, then be sure that they read and sign the waiver form in case of accident." Accident. My mouth dried up just thinking about it.

My only hope was that my parents would say no.

Chapter 18

I brought up the subject late that night, when I knew my parents would be tired and less enthusiastic. "Oh, by the way, some kids from our class are going skiing. I have to get you to sign this sheet to say if you don't want me to go. It's expensive, and I don't mind at all if you say no. Those of us who don't go skiing will stay in the school library that day . . ."

"I think it would be great," said Mom. "I'm sure Susan and Ben will be sending Diane . . ." She stopped abruptly and looked down. "I think it would be great if you tried skiing, Keri. The mountains are very beautiful, and a school trip like that can be so much fun."

"But it costs a lot . . ."

Dad smiled. "Oh, I think we can scrape the money together."

"But . . ."

"Gee, I wish *our* class could go skiing," said Colleen.

"Too bad," I snarled at her. "I don't want to go."

"Why not?" asked Dad.

"Because I'll fall down the mountain and break my neck. Skiing is dangerous, you know. Look, it even says on the permission sheet about accidents and death . . ."

Dad looked exasperated. "Keri, why do you have to be afraid of everything? Look at Colleen . . ."

"Maybe she just doesn't have the brains to be scared."

He folded the newspaper and glared. "Enough of that, young lady!" He took a deep breath. "Look, Keri, you withdrew from the elections because you were afraid of running or losing or whatever. We'll never understand that. It's high time you started doing some of the things that you're scared of."

I turned to Mom. "Please. I just don't want to go. Please."

Mom looked at Dad, then avoided my eyes, but spoke gently. "You might like skiing. This is a perfect chance to try it."

Sure, a perfect chance to make a fool of myself falling down all day in front of my classmates. A perfect chance to break my neck or maybe even die, falling down the mountain.

Anyway, in the end they insisted that I go. I couldn't believe how eagerly my own loving parents would sign that waiver about accidents or death, and send their terrified daughter to certain disaster.

For the first time ever I found myself envying Martha Miller and Harvey Round. Their permission sheets had been returned marked no.

I didn't even have the consolation of getting a new ski outfit like all the other girls. Well, not all the others. But Diane, of course, and Karen, Natalie, and Theresa. They shopped proudly for their new outfits and boasted about the prices.

I asked Mom, "What am I going to wear? We can't afford a new ski outfit for me just for one day. Maybe I'd better not go . . ."

Mom smiled wryly. "I've been thinking of that, Keri. I phoned Susan this morning and she said you could wear Diane's old ski suit. It's as good as new. And it's pink, your favourite colour."

Since the elections, Diane, Karen, Theresa, and Natalie had avoided me, but it didn't bother me not to have their company. In fact, it was like peace after a storm, a time of rest.

One snowy recess afternoon I looked out the window. "Steve, I'm so scared of this ski trip."

"Some bears look more ferocious, but you just jump higher over them."

"Jump? I'm going to stand there petrified in front of the whole class."

"They'll all be off on different slopes," he said. "Slopes are always colour-coded: the black ones are the hardest, blue are easier, and green are the very easiest except for bunny hills. That's where you'll learn." He grinned. "Not even Diane's going to stand around watching you. She'll be so busy on the black slopes skiing, and showing off her new ski suit to all the guys, that she won't have any time to see what you're doing. And I'll go with you to start you off. Don't worry, you'll manage better than you think."

"But I've always been a failure at everything."

"I once heard a saying–'Success is just failure turned inside out.' "

"What's that supposed to mean?"

"You think about it, Keri."

It had been snowing almost all week, and everything was starting to look wintery, like a Christmas card.

Many afternoons Steve swooshed through the snow on his cross-country skis to our place. Then we'd saddle the horses and ride through the soft white powder in the fields. Colleen always let him borrow Pony Bill and I rode Fancy. It was strange to look down on a guy who was so much taller than me.

One afternoon Steve asked, "Would Colleen mind if I tried to canter Pony Bill?"

"Of course not."

Away he went, his arms flapping, his legs dragging through the snow. He turned Pony Bill and galloped back, whooping, his face alive with excitement. Pony Bill was enjoying himself too, prancing, ready for more. Steve pulled to a stop beside me. "Keri, why don't you give it a try? The snow's soft if you do fall."

I looked down. The snow still seemed far away, and underneath it was rock-hard frozen ground.

"Come on. Try. You did get used to galloping on Sandy and you liked it. You'd get to like it on Fancy too. Just give it a try. It's so much fun."

"I thought you understood me, Steve. But now you're pushing me just like everybody else. My stomach is always in knots these days worrying about our stupid ski trip, and here you are bugging me about this."

I turned Fancy sharply and headed towards the barn. Steve called, "Keri, wait. I'm sorry."

That was the last time he tried to talk me into cantering.

The next afternoon he galloped on Fancy, and liked that even better than on Pony Bill. I stood beside Pony Bill, holding his reins, with my arm around his neck, imagining that he was smaller and white and oh, so gentle, as I watched Fancy race across the snowy field with Steve balancing as though he had done this forever. Tears freeze on your face if it's cold enough.

The next week a chinook wind moved in, melting all the snow to mud, which eventually dried in the next few days of warm friendly weather. I started to hope that all the snow would melt in the mountains too, and the ski trip would have to be postponed.

One noon hour Steve and I stood in the hallway talking and laughing, when I noticed Diane watching us intently, thinking deeply, almost as though she were seeing us for the first time. As my eyes met hers she looked away, but a knot gripped my stomach. I knew Diane had just hatched an idea.

It didn't take long to find out what that idea was. As I turned from my locker, she sidled up to Steve. "Stevie, you're so smart, do you think you could help me with my math for a few minutes? I just can't seem to get this one problem."

"Well, uh. I guess so."

Within a few minutes Diane and Steve were sitting in the classroom, side by side, and she was leaning much closer than necessary to watch him work out an algebra problem. Just before the bell rang, she said, "Gee, thanks so much. Stevie, you're great." She put her hand on his arm and laid her head against his shoulder just for a second but I knew that it was long enough for him to smell her perfume and to feel the softness of her hair against his face.

She noticed me watching and smiled sweetly. "Oh, hi, Keri."

The next few days I helplessly watched a campaign unrivalled in any election. At first Steve tried to avoid her, and I wasn't too worried. But as each day passed he seemed to resist less and less. She walked beside him, she asked his opinion on everything, she giggled at his jokes, she fluttered her eyelashes when he spoke seriously.

Over and over I wondered why he couldn't see that Diane was getting involved with him just to hurt me? But then terror would grip. What if she wasn't doing this to get revenge on me? What if she really did like him? That would be worse, so much worse.

Then one afternoon on the bus, Jennifer sat beside Linda, and Diane sat alone behind them. When Steve walked on the bus, Diane slid over and called, "Hey, Stevie, come sit here." He hesitated, but then did sit beside her, his shoulders tight.

Ron climbed on the bus, raised his eyebrows, and walked back to sit beside me. He didn't say anything about Steve or Diane, but I could see him watching them.

The next morning I heard Diane talking to Steve about horses, and realized that Steve had been to Diane's place to ride King.

At noon that day, I noticed Roxanne sadly watching Diane flirting with Steve. As I walked out into the hallway, she caught up to me. "So, Keri, do you think we'll have snow for the ski trip?"

The words flew out. "I sure hope not!"

She cringed, and I felt badly. "Sorry. It's just that I've never skied before, and I'm kinda scared of it."

Her eyes looked soft, hardly focussing. "I remember how terrified I was when I first tried. My Aunt Agnes took me. It's scary, but it really is worth it. She took me a few more times and I really got to like skiing. It's peaceful and beautiful up there in the white mountains. That was a long time ago."

She blinked, and seemed to come back to reality. "Maybe I could help you get started, give you a few pointers . . ."

"No, it's OK. Steve promised . . ." I had blurted out the words without even realizing they were coming.

"Steve promised to help you?" Roxanne spoke so softly. "He will then, don't worry. I don't think he'll break a promise like that. Not to you. And, Keri, don't worry too much about Diane. She just . . ."

"Excuse me," I said, my voice cold as ice. "I have to go see Mrs. Pratt about some science questions."

It was true what Jennifer had said. When someone really got to know me, then that person didn't like me any more. No wonder I was scared to get close to anyone. It had happened with Diane, with Jennifer, with many others in the past. But I had never meant to let Steve know me so well, had never planned to get so close. As the aching days passed I became more determined that I wouldn't let it happen again. Even with Sandy, I'd allowed myself to become much too close.

The weather had been beautiful for over a week. One morning Mr. Korban commented, "Sure is nice warm weather for November. But I'm afraid we might have to postpone our ski trip. I hear there's hardly any snow left on the mountains." That afternoon it started to snow heavily.

Within a few days, the ski slopes opened and Diane came back from a weekend of skiing with her parents to report that ski conditions were good.

"All systems go!" Gerald whooped.

Very early Friday morning our parents drove us to the school, and in the darkness we hurried onto the bus. Diane sat beside Steve toward the middle of the bus. Ron sat three seats behind them, and asked me to sit with him. I was glad for his kindness.

With the two classes together on the bus, the ride to Banff seemed short. Lots of talking and flirting and laughter. The two teachers and the four parents sat at the front, visiting, and didn't seem to mind the bedlam going on behind them.

Greg Robinson, the handsome vice-president of the student council, was sitting with his friend Lawrence in front of Diane and Steve. Greg and Lawrence turned around a lot to talk to them. By the time the sun came up, highlighting Greg's face with gold and orange, it seemed as though he was talking much more to Diane than to Steve. I wondered how Steve felt.

When we got out of the bus I stood in a daze watching the kids unload their ski equipment. Greg and Lawrence hung around, blatantly admiring Diane in her gorgeous new tangerine ski suit. Diane glanced at me and said, "Gee Keri, my old pink outfit doesn't look too bad on you." Then she turned to Steve and Greg. "Well, guys, let's hit those black runs right away."

Steve hesitated. "Uh, I promised to help Keri get started skiing. She's never tried it before . . ."

"You mean you're going to waste this gorgeous day babysitting on the bunny slopes?" Then she realized that Steve was frowning and had moved over towards me. I watched her face. It changed immediately, as though being put into a different gear. "Sorry, just joking."

"Steve, it's OK." I wished fervently that I was in the library with Martha Miller and Harvey Round. "You go ahead with them. I'll be all right."

"No, Keri, I promised to help you and I really want to."

Diane smiled sweetly at him. "I'll try a few runs and come back for you later, Stevie." She wrapped her arm around his waist for a second before she headed over to the chairlift with the others.

Splendid in their new ski outfits, Natalie, Karen, and Theresa strolled by, chatting and laughing with some of the kids from Mr. Ross's class. "Hey, Steve," Karen called, "want to come with us? We're headed for the green runs first to loosen up our muscles."

"I'll be coming in a little while. . . ."

Steve took me to the ski shop and helped me rent all the things. Len, Roxanne, and several others were there to rent equipment too. They quickly picked out what they wanted and headed for the slopes. But before she left, Roxanne touched my arm and said, "Good luck."

"Thanks," I mumbled, hardly paying attention to her.

Steve helped me fasten the ski boots, big awkward boots that hold your feet forward like they were set in concrete.

I balanced against Steve to put on the skis. Like prison doors, the safety release mechanisms slammed shut. "They're adjusted loose for beginners," Steve said. "They must release easily if you fall, so you don't break a leg." He grinned. "Us experienced show-offs adjust ours tighter so they don't release when we're turning really hard. Only trouble with that is sometimes they don't release on a fall, and we could break a leg."

I stood there in the brilliant sunshine, my eyes scrunched against the dazzling snow. Being on skis felt like standing up in a canoe, that same unstable, we're-going-to-tip-over feeling. I just wanted to sit down.

There was hardly any slope from the rental shop to the T-bar, but wouldn't you know it, my skis slid out from under me, and I fell in the hard-packed snow.

I lay there watching a little kid glide smoothly by me. Steve pulled me up and brushed the snow off Diane's old ski suit.

"Steve, you'd better go on without me."

"No way." He grinned. "You need me."

We joined the line at the Sunny T-bar that would take us

to the beginner slope. Its name was Sunnyside. Sunnyside up, I thought. And easy over.

There weren't many kids from our trip in that line because nearly all of them already knew how to ski.

I watched the people ahead take the moving bar from the attendant and glide up the hill. "Be sure you get a good grip on the bar. Keep your knees flexed. Lean back against the bar but don't try to sit on it." All too soon it was our turn.

I grabbed the bar below Steve's hand. We lurched forward. My skis slid out behind and down I went, flat on my face in the snow.

Steve pulled me up, brushed me off, and smiled tenderly. That smile of his could melt an iceberg. Amazed, I found myself trying the T-bar again, and this time I kept my feet underneath me and made it to the top of Sunnyside slope.

The rental shop seemed so far down. My face stiffened as the blood drained away. "Steve, I can't do it. I can't ski down there."

"Well," he said softly, "just stand here for a while and get used to it before we start. There's no other way down."

Chapter 19

"OK, you start out by learning to snowplough," Steve said. He pointed his skis like a V-shaped plough and headed down the hill. "Now, you try."

I turned my toes inward and skidded awkwardly over the hard-packed snow, delighted to find myself still upright. Even better, the ski shop had moved a bit closer.

Smiling and calling encouragement, Steve skied smoothly in a serpentine pattern along beside me.

About halfway down the hill I stopped. "Wow. The front of my legs are aching."

"That's from snowploughing. Snowploughing isn't much fun. It's just a way of getting down a hill. Now try keeping your skis parallel and turning them from side to side like I'm doing. It feels better, and it *is* fun."

Fun. OK, I'd try that. But I made only one turn before earth and sky swung around and changed places. Steve pulled me up. Again I tried, and again I fell, this time sliding a bit before I could dig my skis in to stop. I panicked. "Steve," I cried, "what if I fall and start sliding all the way down the hill and can't stop?"

"Don't worry. This slope is much too gradual. That could only happen on really steep slopes like the black runs. And I don't think you'll be tackling those for a while."

He helped me to my feet and I tried again. Another few turns and down I went, my left leg wrenching as I fell. With a loud click, the safety mechanism released. That foot felt so free, I wished I could take the other ski off and slide on my rear end all the way down.

Balancing against Steve, I shoved my boot back onto the ski. The safety mechanism imprisoned me again.

After a few more turns and a lot more falls, we were almost three-quarters of the way down the hill. The rental shop looked close. I started to relax a bit, and managed the last part of the bunny hill without hitting the snow, making turns that even resembled S-shapes.

Up we went again. This time I fell only twice on my way down. "You know, Steve, the worst part for me is the top of the hill. Once I get over halfway down it doesn't seem so bad. But it's so awful at the top."

Steve smiled. "Sure wouldn't want to take you on black runs for a while." He looked at me. "You look cold. Do you want to go back to the lodge to warm up with a cup of hot chocolate?"

"You bet."

"Great. First one down pays the bill." He pushed off, and within a few seconds was standing at the bottom watching me weave my way down. "You see some pretty ski bunnies on a bunny slope," he said, grinning.

After a few minutes rest, we tried Sunnyside again. I was getting used to it and starting to feel guilty for taking so much of Steve's trip. Then I saw Diane riding the T-bar, and wished I could take up his whole day.

"Hi," Diane called, stopping sideways with elegant style. "The black slopes are fantastic today. Everybody's asking where you are. When are you coming, Steve?"

"Pretty soon. Keri's doing really well. But she needs to try Sunnyside a few more times. Then she can tackle Wiwaxy from Glacier Chair."

"Oh,Stevie, come on. She'll be OK. The Back Bowl and Larch areas are gorgeous today."

I looked from Diane to Steve. It would hurt so much to see them ski off together. Yet it wasn't right to monopolize any more of his time.

"Steve, you go ahead," I forced myself to say, but I almost hugged him when he shook his head and said, "I just can't leave Keri here alone. Not till she gets some more confidence. Then I'll come and ski with you guys. Honest, I will."

Diane pouted. "Have it your way." We watched her zoom down the slope and join the line for the Olympic Chair.

This seemed like the time for visitors. Down the hill came Ron Vander. He skidded to a stop.

"What are you doing here, Vander?" Steve asked.

"Oh, I saw Diane head this way and figured she might get her hooks into you, and then Keri'd be left without a teacher. So I thought I might have to give her some genuine professional ski lessons."

Steve looked slightly annoyed. "Well, you can see that I'm still here." Then he chuckled. "What would a motorcycle nut know about giving ski lessons?"

"Oh, me and my old man go skiing when the snow's too deep for our bikes. Have to get our thrills somehow, you know. And my old man, he paid for me to have lessons from real live ski instructors. So I know how they learn you. Step back and let a pro take over. Miss Andersen, show me some turns."

I tried a couple of turns, my muscles tight.

Ron shook his head. "Terrible. Terrible. Bend your knees more, kid, like you're praying."

I couldn't help but laugh. "I am praying."

Ron wrinkled his face. "Well, if I was God, I wouldn't be too impressed. Lean forward way more. Kneel. Right onto the front of your boots."

He peered at me sideways, squinting his eyes. "Always put all your weight – skinny as you are – on your downhill ski. Yep. Much better. See what a good teacher can do. Lomar, you're going to have to find yourself a different job.

"Now, Keri, my girl, you want to turn left. Pretend that there's a dimmer switch button under the big toe on your right foot, and press down hard on it." I tried, and without any effort, found myself turning. Amazing!

After a few minutes of Ron's pointers, I was actually enjoying myself as I twisted down the hill.

When we stood at the bottom of Sunnyside, I looked up, thrilled to think that I had skied that slope without fear.

Ron turned to Steve. "She's doing good. I think we should take her on something a bit more challenging. The next 'green' slope. Onward to the Glacier Chair and Wiwaxy Run. Onward and upward."

The idea of something steeper, something higher, made me pale. Ron studied my face. "It's the height that does you in, isn't it? You can do it, kid. You've got the world's greatest ski instructor here."

I looked away.

"Think of the scenery. Mountains and forests and big valleys. Not like this boring place with only the ski shop and T-bar and dozens of clumsy beginners for scenery."

I laughed, but it came out high and squeaky.

"Old Steve here, he can sit with you on the chair and hold your hand and calm your troubled mind. Real romantic. And remember the gorgeous view."

"Keri," Steve said, "you can do it. Come on. Give it a try."

I was cold and tired. If only I had the nerve to say no to them. Desperately I longed to hand in my equipment and spend the rest of the day relaxing in the ski lodge.

But I felt so mixed up. It would be good to learn to ski. Maybe somehow, someday, I could ski with Steve, really ski with him, not just keep him back like this.

I swallowed hard. "OK, let's go."

We joined the line to the chair lift. I watched people get

on. Those chairs kept moving! You had to move sideways as the chair glided in behind you, and sit down at just the right time. It looked horrible. I fought my overwhelming urge to run back to the rental shop.

"Me first," Ron said. "See you at the top."

He slid easily into the chair with the guy ahead in the line, and turned back to wave at us as they were lifted into the air.

Steve gripped my arm. "Get ready. Here we go." I shuffled ahead with him. Then he pulled me sideways. "Keri, look behind. Sit back. Now."

The chair hit my legs and I plopped into it. Not too bad. At least I hadn't fallen.

But then I looked down.

I had thought Fancy was high above the ground! Now there was at least ten times that stretch of empty space between my feet and the mountain side. My stomach lurched, threatening to empty lunch on Diane's old pink ski suit. I gulped and looked ahead.

"You OK?" Steve asked.

I nodded. Ron was looking back at me, making a funny face. But I couldn't laugh.

Steve understood. "Look across, over there, Keri. That's Olympic Chair. It takes you to the very top of Wiwaxy Run. The view from the top is incredible. When we get off this chair, we join the bottom two-thirds of Wiwaxy." I wasn't answering, but he knew that I wanted him to talk. It helped keep my mind from the chasm below.

"Now, to get off the chair, you slide to the edge, push yourself off, and then ski out of the way," said Steve.

He did it easily, but I landed on my back in the snow, staring up at the next chair swinging towards me. Two women slid off the chair, speeding down the ramp, straight at me. I screamed. They swooshed by, just missing my head. Snow sprayed into my eyes and mouth. Steve grabbed my hand and yanked me away just as the next couple slid off their chair.

I was trembling.

Steve looked at me gently. "I think it's harder to get off those crazy lift chairs than to learn to ski."

The lodge was far below, tiny as a toy, with miniature people moving around it.

"Steve . . ." I breathed, clinging to him.

Ron skied over to us. "Those ladies just about got you, eh? Well, the tough part's over now. Let's go."

What could I do but follow? We skied down a slight slope and turned into a tree-lined trail that curved and then started to look terribly steep. My knees were shaking.

But after a little while we came to a meadow with a gentle, wide slope skirted by trees. "Like it?" Ron called over his shoulder.

"Yeah, it's beautiful here." I could see soft blue mountains far across the valley, but because of the big spruce trees and the gentle slope, there wasn't that terrifying feeling of height. I was getting colder and more tired all the time, but still had to admit it was fun.

Ron and Steve skied patiently beside me, and I began to relax. The lodge was getting closer. Much closer.

Yeah, this was nice. But then we turned a corner and my heart seemed to stop.

The trail fell. Almost straight down.

I stood petrified. "I can't make that. I thought Wiwaxy was supposed to be a green slope. Green for easy."

"It is. You should see the black slopes." Ron grinned. "You can do it. Don't look down. Don't even think of going down. Just work your way across, then turn, and go across again. Just zig-zag real wide all the way down. And remember to turn your skis anytime you get going too fast. That'll slow you right away."

He seemed so sure. I took a deep breath and started, a snail on snow. A few zig-zags later I realized Ron was right. I could do this, if I just took it a little at a time. Turn. Straight across. Turn. . . .

I turned too quickly. My skis started to slide, pointed forward, pulling me faster, faster. I was hurtling down, straight down. . . .

"Turn!" Ron shouted. "Turn your skis!"

But the skis were controlling me, like two runaway horses, with me trying to stand between them, one foot on each saddle. I couldn't turn, and my skis slid faster, rattling along over the hard-packed snow, down, down, the ground blurring, my eyes stinging in the wind.

"Press on your left toe!" Ron screamed. But I lurched my whole body instead, and felt myself flip through the air. Almost in slow motion I fell, sliding, tumbling, twisting. . . .

At last there was no more motion, and I lay in the snow. There was a horrible sound, a shrieking, like a wild, hurt animal.

The screaming echoed off the mountain, back to my gaping mouth. My eyes felt glued open, unable to focus.

Chapter 20

Strong arms were shaking me. "Keri, Keri." Steve and Ron were calling me. I had to stop the screaming. I looked up into their saucer eyes and lay in the snow, crying, shaking. They kept calling my name, but I didn't care about them any more.

We weren't anywhere near the bottom yet. I struggled to sit up and felt the pull of that awful slope. Never. I could never ever make it down.

"Keri, are you hurt?" Steve looked so concerned. I stared at him numbly, and then noticed one leg tucked backward underneath me. The ski lay in the soft snow beside the run. I pulled my leg, as though in slow motion, and moved it forward, lifting it. Nothing broken.

They looked so relieved, but I didn't share the feeling. I could never ever get down.

A scream was rising again in my throat. I pushed it back but it waited, ready to drown me. Ron kept twisting his hands around his ski pole. "Keri, you ready to get up and try again?" The scream clawed its way up, but I closed my mouth, swallowed, and stared down with glazed eyes. Straight down. So steep.

Ron bent and grabbed my arm to pull me up. "Come on, kid, it's not as bad as it looks."

I shrieked and pulled away. Steve sat down beside me. "Listen, Keri. You have to do this." I leaned my face into the coldness of the snow and sobbed.

Steve stood up, took my arm, and before I could protest, had pulled me to my feet. I realized that my knee and hip hurt, but that was nothing compared with how it would hurt to fall the next time, or the next.

It seemed even steeper now that I was standing. Ron brought my ski over and lifted my foot into it. Slam. Trapped. I thought of all the stories I'd read and heard about ski accidents. Broken bones, broken backs, wheelchairs, crippled for life.

"Keri." It was Ron speaking. Softer than I'd ever heard him speak. A pleading tone of voice. "Keri, see that big tree right across there? Well, there's a great-looking guy waiting for you over there, hiding behind it. You can't keep him waiting much longer."

"Yeah." Steve pulled his mouth into a smile. "Let's just ski over there and see if he's better looking than Ron or me."

Steve started off, skiing as though in slow motion, and looked back at me. "Come on, Keri, follow me. We'll see if this guy is worth your time."

As though pulled by a string, I pointed my skis towards that tree and let them glide along, ever so slightly down, slowly, slowly, across the run, straight towards that tree.

Just before he reached it, Steve turned effortlessly. Now he was below me and I felt terror rise again.

Ron called, "Keri, there's a bug under your right foot. Step on it with your big toe. Squish it. With that big toe. Hard, real hard!"

I obeyed and felt my skis turn smoothly. "Oh, look," Steve called, "now there's an even better-looking guy across there on the other side by that big mound of snow. Let's head straight for him."

Ron followed along behind me. When I reached the edge, he said, "Now squish that bug with your left big toe. Harder."

I turned, but my feet slid unevenly, and I fell and started sliding. "Dig the sides of your skis into the snow," Ron yelled. It worked. My body swerved and stopped abruptly, lying in the snowbank.

Steve pulled me up again.

I stood trembling while they gently brushed the snow off my face. I glanced down the slope again and wished I hadn't. "It's no good, you guys. I can't do it. I can't get down there."

Steve ignored my protests. "Now, see that little tree straight across on the other side? Head for it."

Ron grinned wickedly and opened his eyes wide. "Good grief, there's a *naked* guy hiding behind *that* tree, Keri. You'd better get over there quick."

I couldn't help laughing. And I made it across and managed the turn. The next part of the slope was even steeper, I could tell, even though they wouldn't let me look down. "Hey, Keri," said Steve, "right across there by that snowbank. Look. There's Mr. Fisher. Your very favourite teacher. We'd better get over there right away, or we might miss out on one of his exciting worksheets."

When I made that turn, I looked down.

"It's not far now to the bottom of this bad slope," Ron said, "and then the rest of the way is easier, much easier. Honest."

I found myself smiling. "You guys wouldn't lie to me."

"Oh, never. Not us." Steve grinned. "Every word we utter is gospel truth."

"That's right," Ron said. "Hey, look over there on the other side. A big heap of money, just lying there in the snow, waiting for you to claim it."

A couple more turns and we were down that bad slope. "You did it!" Steve shouted.

I looked at the two grinning faces. "Nope, you guys did it." We all laughed.

The ski lodge looked much bigger. My legs ached. I was so cold that my teeth were clattering, but I didn't care.

When we finally reached the lodge, Ron said, "Well, Lomar, you'd better take the lady in and buy her lunch to celebrate. I'm off to the Back Bowl. No rest for the wicked. Less for the lousy."

I grinned at him. "For a wicked and lousy guy, you're a pretty good ski instructor. Ron, thanks so much. Why don't we all have lunch together?"

"Naw, eating is for mere mortals. I've got some skiing to do. And if the ol' body does give in and beg for food, there's always Temple Lodge on the other side of the mountain. Don't worry about me."

"Steve, then why don't you go along with him now? I'll be fine. Honest."

"Too hungry. Got to eat now. Sorry, Keri, you can't get rid of me that easily. See you, Vander. You did OK, you know."

After lunch, I said, "Now, Steve, you are going to the other side of the mountain to ski."

"You can't just sit here in the lodge all afternoon."

"Why not? It's nice in here. I'm going to sit and do absolutely nothing for a while. Then I might try Sunnyside a couple of times on my own." That was a lie; I had no intention of leaving my beautifully safe lodge chair. But surely lies you tell to keep someone from worrying aren't really lies at all. "I just need to be alone for a while, please, Steve. And you need to get back to those Larch and Bowl runs that I keep hearing about."

"It's spectacular back there," he said, almost reverently. "You'd love it. Someday, I hope you can ski well enough for the two of us to go together. It's so beautiful that you'd think you'd died and gone to heaven."

A few minutes after Steve left I heard a familiar laugh and looked up, startled. It was Diane walking in with Karen, Greg, and Lawrence. They were talking loudly, having a great time.

I wished I could hide. They were headed towards the cafeteria line, and would have to walk right past me.

"Oh, hi there, Keri!" Diane called. "Having a good time, are you? Where's Steve?"

"Out skiing."

"Yeah, I knew he'd eventually get tired of babysitting. Guess what? You're not the only chicken around here. You should see old Roxanne Campbell up on Grizzly Bowl, sitting in the snow, staring down the mountain side. She reminded me of another wimp I used to know, a baby who got herself stuck way up in a tree."

They all laughed loudly and started to walk on. Trembling, I forced myself to call after them, "What happened to her? Why is she sitting there?"

Diane smirked. "Don't know. We never stopped to visit. I guess she probably had a good fall and lost her nerve. Looks like she'll be up there for a while before she crawls down that slope." The laughter became more raucous.

Anger swelled in my chest and I was amazed to hear myself ask, "Why didn't you guys help her?"

"Aw," Diane answered, "she can get down. It's just one short bad slope and then it joins Wiwaxy."

"Yeah," Greg said, "the rest of the trail is easy, though she probably doesn't know it from where she is."

Diane laughed. "She'll probably make it down when she gets cold enough. Grizzly isn't used very much, so she'll get a little lonely. But eventually somebody might come along and talk her down. Anyway, she's got the scenery to watch while she's waiting."

"So why don't you guys go up and help her?" The words tumbled out by themselves.

"You've got to be kidding. We can't go rescuing people every time they get a little scared. Might make them into real cowards like somebody we know. It would be good for weird old Roxanne to help herself down. She'd see what she's able to do. Anyhow, right after lunch we're going to the Back

Bowls and Larch. Talk about scenery! It's incredible back there."

"By the way, Keri," Karen said, gritting her teeth, "don't you go bothering Mr. Korban about poor little Roxanne. He might wonder how you knew where she was. You wouldn't want to get us into trouble for leaving her stranded, would you?" Karen turned to Lawrence. "You really have to watch this kid, you know. Getting people in trouble is her hobby."

They all chortled and joined the cafeteria line. I sat looking out the window, watching the skiers whiz down the hill, unable to think of anything but Roxanne stranded somewhere up there.

After they finished their lunch, the four walked past me again. "I've got a good idea, Keri," Diane sneered. "Why don't *you* go up there and talk Roxanne down." They all laughed.

Time seemed endless after that. If only Ron and Steve were around. They could talk her down just like they had done for me. If only there was some way of getting a message to them. But all the good skiers from the trip seemed to have gone to the north face for the rest of the afternoon.

I sat by the window, watching. She must soon come down. She knew how to ski. It's just to get over that terrible helplessness that comes with panic. Oh, Roxanne, try. You'll make it. Get up and try again.

I walked out to the front of the lodge and studied the huge map that showed all the runs. I saw Wiwaxy marked with a green circle beside it. Green for most easy. I had done the bottom two-thirds of it.

The map showed the Olympic Chair. Off to the left of Olympic Chair was the very top of Wiwaxy run. Still marked green. Off to the right of Olympic Chair was Grizzly Bowl. Grizzly was a short run. Yes, very short. Then it joined Wiwaxy. Good old green Wiwaxy. But Grizzly Bowl was marked with a black diamond. Black diamond. Most difficult.

Then I saw Mr. Korban. Gliding down the hill, he turned effortlessly and headed towards Olympic Chair. I couldn't tell him anything about Roxanne. But what if I just chatted with him? Maybe I could mention the pretty view at the top of Grizzly and ask him if he'd ever skied that run. Maybe he'd try it and find Roxanne himself.

I ran, as fast as possible in the heavy, awkward ski boots, sliding and tripping until I got to Olympic Chair. Then I pulled up short. I really hadn't talked to Mr. Korban since I'd bowled him over, charging out of the boys' bathroom. The memory of that awful moment hadn't faded a bit. But I had to do something about Roxanne.

"Hi, Mr. Korban," I said, staring past his left shoulder.

"Oh. Hi, Keri." He looked down. "What are you doing out here without skis?"

"Uh, just taking a rest, walking around. You know. Getting the pins and needles out of my feet." I took a deep breath. "Are you enjoying your skiing?"

"Sure am." He had moved out of the line to talk to me. "The skiing is great today. I've been trying all the different runs." I couldn't believe it. Here was my chance.

"Have you ever tried Grizzly Bowl? I hear it's really pretty up there."

"Yeah, I did once last year. But it's not really worth it because it's such a short run. Hardly anybody bothers with it. It's a killer if you're not a good skier. And if you're a good skier it just takes about two minutes to zoom down it."

I stood, stunned.

"So, Keri, how has your day been going?"

"Pretty good, I guess." My voice was feeble. "Well, I'd better let you get back to skiing."

He joined the line and waved at me when the chair lifted him.

I waited almost an hour. Still no Roxanne.

I thought of how Roxanne had the courage to talk to me in the bathroom when I ran out of Mr. Fisher's classroom. And I thought with guilt of all the times that she had tried to befriend me and I rejected her attempts at friendship.

I watched the slopes for a good skier from our class. If only

I could get a message to Ron or Steve that they should come back to me. They'd be here right away.

I looked at Grizzly on the map again. A black diamond run. Most difficult.

I waited longer. Mr. Korban said it was a killer for anyone but good skiers. A killer.

But it was short. And then it joined Wiwaxy. I had done that part.

Roxanne was sitting there. Crying. Feeling awful. Nobody to care about her. Even if some people were taking Grizzly, they would probably zoom by her so fast that they wouldn't even notice that she was in trouble. They'd just think she was taking a rest.

They wouldn't notice those glassy eyes. Oh, Roxanne, hurry down. You can do it. You have to.

What if she didn't get down before we were ready to leave? We were supposed to be at the bus at 4:30. When Mr. Korban noticed Roxanne missing, would Diane and her crew admit they knew where she was? They would have to. Then they would get into trouble. Good. They deserved it. And Mr. Korban and Ron and Steve could go up the chair to talk Roxanne down.

But then I remembered. The chairs stopped running at four o'clock. It said that on the map. The Olympic Chair stopped running at four o'clock. But surely they would start the chairs again if someone was stuck up there. The ski patrol would go get her. No problem. I looked at my watch. Almost two-thirty. Only an hour and a half. She'd be all right.

But it got dark before five o'clock these days. By the time they got to Roxanne it would be dusk. How horrible to be stuck on a mountain as the sun disappeared. And when they'd be trying to talk her down it would be completely dark.

What if I went up there and tried to talk her down? Now. While it was still light. Just thinking about it made my chest tighten and my legs tremble. No way. I couldn't possibly do it.

Why, oh, why, hadn't I just told Mr. Korban? Facing the

music with Diane and the others would have been easier than facing that black diamond hill.

No. I could never make it down Grizzly. It wouldn't help to have two of us stranded up there. But Roxanne needed someone.

Roxanne had always needed someone. And I had never given anything to anybody. Always worried about myself.

I could do it. I had to do it. I could get her to come down with crazy talk, the way Ron and Steve had helped me. Somehow, I'd be all right. Just talk myself down at the same time.

No, I couldn't.

My hands were shaking. If it was too bad, we could take off our skis and skid down on our bums. I would go up and help her. We'd make it down somehow. I put on my skis. Then I released them and stood horrified, wondering at what I'd almost done.

Hugging skis and poles to my body, I started back towards the lodge. She'd get down. Somehow. Soon.

My eyes scoured the hill, imagining every figure in a green ski suit to be Roxanne. None of them were.

No good. It had to be done. I forced myself to put the skis back on, and with dread, shuffled towards Olympic Chair.

Chapter 21

I rode Olympic lift up to the top, praying, gripping the chair pole, trying not to look down. The girl who sat beside me chatted lightly, totally unaware of my turmoil. Somehow I got off the chair and down the ramp without falling. A good omen.

Here it was. The turn to the right would bring me down Grizzly Bowl. But the turn to the left would bring me down Wiwaxy. I could still change my mind. I looked to the right. The black diamond sign. A killer. I had to forget this crazy attempt at heroics and ski off to the left. To get myself all the way down Wiwaxy would be enough of a challenge. The top of Wiwaxy was supposed to be quite steep for a green run.

I stood, hating myself, already knowing which way I would take. Roxanne would get down somehow. Maybe she was already at the lodge. I couldn't risk getting stuck by myself on Grizzly.

But Roxanne needed me.

I turned and pushed off on my poles towards black diamond Grizzly. On wobbly legs I skied a little further down, past some trees, and then I saw the view. It was everything they had said it was. I was standing at the rim of a huge white half-bowl. Far across the valley stretched purple mountains, capped with dazzling white snow. The parking lot was so far away that I could hardly see the vehicles.

I forced my eyes to look down into the bowl. Straight down. Steep like a cliff. Nothing to block the view. Just a few small trees hung over the edges, their toes clinging desperately to the windswept rocks.

And to my horror, I couldn't see Roxanne. She had made it down. I was stuck on a black run all by myself. All alone. "Roxanne," I muttered, "I'm going to kill you. I come all the way up this stupid mountain to rescue you, and you don't even have the decency to be here."

Everything was so tiny, so far away. If only I could ski with my eyes closed. Shaking violently, I pushed off as gently as possible and panicked at the sudden acceleration. I sat down at the edge in the deep snow to catch my breath. Then somehow I forced my aching legs to stand again, and tried another turn.

With a violent lurch, I lost my balance, flipped, and landed in deep powdery snow, my legs crumpling and twisting. Both skis released. All above was snowbank and sky. The arms and back of my ski suit were crammed full of snow. My scream echoed around me, slicing the air. Quit screaming. It only makes things worse.

My heart was pounding so furiously it seemed to choke me. Alone. All alone in this nightmare.

I'd never get down. Had to climb up. Back to Wiwaxy. I struggled to put my skis on. I couldn't go back without them. They were my curse but my only salvation. Without them I could never make it all the way back to the lodge.

I fought to climb that hill, leaning at the edge of the world, my arms in the snow, my hands pawing to pull me up, digging in the edges of my skis, one foot at a time. It's hard to work muscles that are shaking so violently.

The snow inside Diane's pink ski suit had started to melt, making me even colder.

This was taking forever, and I was getting too weak. Why not remove my skis and try climbing without them? My clumsy numb hands released the bindings. Carrying the awkward skis and poles, I battled gravity and snow.

No good. I clung to a stunted spruce and struggled to put my skis on again. It took much longer this time.

Then I leaned my whole body into the snow wall, into the side of the bowl, and clawed up into its softness, my legs growing weaker, each tiny step taking longer, gaining less. It wasn't working. I would have to go down. Down.

I looked over the edge and felt a sudden, sickening pull. The bottom of the valley seemed to be reaching for me. My stomach tightened and then heaved, emptying lunch onto the spotless white snow, masking the fragrant scent of spruce.

Then I collapsed, hardly enough strength left to sob.

Maybe I could take my skis off and slide down. But the snow was so soft and deep, not at all packed like the well-used runs. I would just sink into the snow, wasting what little energy I had left.

Somehow I had to ski down. A killer. That's what Mr. Korban had said. But so short. Two minutes for a good skier. Just a little ways to Wiwaxy. If I could just get started, go easy, go slowly. . . .

Trying not to look too far ahead, I forced myself to concentrate on all the things Ron and Steve had taught me. Slowly, slowly. Straight across. Don't look down. Slowly. Push on your big toe. Now straight across again. Slowly. My twitching, burning muscles begged to be pushed no further. Every time I fell, more snow packed into my ski suit. Inside, my clothes were saturated with sweat and melted snow.

I turned a slight corner and there she was. Sitting by the edge of the run in the deep snow, hugging her legs, gazing across the valley, like a statue.

"Roxanne!" My shriek made her turn. And I saw her face white as snow, white as Sandy. . . .

The slope was impossibly steep. I lost my balance and fell, sliding, down, down. But it was as though I could hear Ron yell, "Dig in the sides of your skis!" I ploughed to a stop in the deep powdery snow near the motionless girl.

"Roxanne." She didn't answer, just looked at me like a wounded trapped animal, then leaned her head against her knees.

"Roxanne, can you get up?" She didn't move. "Please try. You have to." I took her arm and tried to pull her up, but she was a dead weight.

I panicked. It had been bad enough to get myself this far. I still couldn't even see Wiwaxy. How could I get Roxanne down? This was more than I could handle.

I needed to talk to her, to reason with her, but I was so scared for both of us, that the words wouldn't come out at all. Like trying to talk in a nightmare. Or like trying to run in a nightmare. I made the attempt, but nothing was working.

So I reached and put my arm around her. And she grabbed me by the shoulders, clutching frantically as though she would crush me.

Then she leaned her head against my chest and sobbed as though she would break. No one had ever leaned on me like that.

"Roxanne, stand up. Try." She didn't answer, just kept crying. I'd have to go for help. Somehow, I could make it down to the lodge. Mr. Korban would have to be told the whole story. Facing Diane and the others seemed mild now compared to trying to get Roxanne and me down this mountain.

"Roxanne, I have to leave you. I'm going to get help."

She shook her head and whimpered, clinging more desperately to me.

It was going to be dark soon. The wind seemed stronger, raw, and icy. We were both shivering uncontrollably. If I left her now, it would be completely dark by the time someone got back to her. And she would be so cold.

"OK, I won't leave you. We're going to make it down together. Come on, stand up."

She didn't respond.

"Now, listen here," I shouted, "because of you I came up here to a blasted black run! And you won't even try to help yourself or me." My chest swelled thick with anger. "I could get killed going down here, killed or crippled for the rest of my life, and you would be to blame!"

Her glassy eyes moved and focussed hard on the snow between us, and her lip started to tremble. "I never asked you to come up here." Then she muttered, "I never asked anything of you."

The words seemed to catch, like a fish hook, in the air. She looked at me, into me. "I never asked anything of you, Keri Andersen. Except to be my friend. But I'm not popular enough to be a friend of yours."

I felt punctured, furious. "Why would anybody want you for a friend? You're always so dismal and dreary!"

She cringed like a whipped dog, but her eyes blazed. "Well, I guess dismal and dreary is better than sucking up to all the popular kids who couldn't care less about you."

My stomach tightened. "Wow. I'm risking my life to help you . . ."

She yelled, "Stop talking about risking your life and getting crippled and all that! Quit it!" Terror had returned to her face. I followed her gaze down the steep slope. No, this wasn't helping.

"I fell," she murmured. "Real bad. Never fell like that before. Couldn't stop. Twisting and rolling and screaming." Her eyes glazed. "I hit that rock. Couldn't get my breath. Like drowning. And I couldn't make my legs move. Like they were tied. Hurting all over. Hurting so bad." She looked up at me frantically. "I can't do it," she cried.

I took a deep breath. "Roxanne," I said gently, "see that little tree over there? Straight across? There's a good-looking guy hiding behind it. Let's ski over there, just straight across to that tree, and see him."

She groaned and turned away from me. Cold, naked terror gripped my mind. I felt like screaming.

Then I remembered. The only time I had really seen those blue-grey eyes sparkle. Her talk in Miss Phillips's class. About the birds.

"Roxanne." I touched her shoulder. "Your special blue jay, the one that's so fussy. He's over there on that little tree, and he hasn't had any dried corn today. He's so hungry. Let's just ski over there and give him some corn."

Her eyes flooded with tears and she clung to me, but she stood up.

I hardly dared breathe.

"Over there," I whispered. "The blue jay. Hungry. Go take him some corn."

Slowly, as though in a trance, she started off. Shaky, unsteady, wobbly. I followed right behind, knowing it wasn't safe to ski so close. When she faltered, I slid around and ahead. It would be better if I could stay just a few lengths in front.

"Come on, Roxanne. He's waiting."

As she reached the tree, I called, "Now there's a bug under your left toe. Squash it. Hard. You can feed it to the woodpecker! Look on the other side. Straight over there. On that crooked tree. A little hungry woodpecker." I pushed off, struggling to get there before she did.

Roxanne turned her skis and headed towards the crooked tree. And then she laughed. It was a trembling laugh, not very strong, but it was a laugh.

It seemed to ring across the valley. A strange new happiness swelled in my chest and lifted me as though I would soar.

I looked down. The slope was even steeper here. Worse than any heights in my cruelest nightmare. "Roxanne," I called, my voice thin and squeaky, "your blue jay has moved. Over there on the other side. Straight across, by all those cute little chickadees. Slowly. Don't scare them. Straight across. We'll take them some sunflower seeds."

Every time we fell, we pulled each other up and started again. Just a few more turns, and then we saw a skier race past on a well-used trail. "Wiwaxy!" I shouted.

We collapsed in the snow, shaking, huddled against the frigid wind. There was still the long run of Wiwaxy, including the terrible place where I'd fallen. How good it would be to lie down right now and sleep.

"Hey, Keri." Roxanne was grinning weakly. "Old Dismal and Dreary here wants to say thanks."

"I'm so sorry I said that . . ."

"Why? It's true. No, it *was* true. I don't feel very dismal and dreary right now." She laughed, and then sighed. "Just tired and weary. Tired and aching all over."

It was almost dark when we got back. The chairs weren't running anymore, and an eerie silence shrouded the hill as the last few skiers glided down.

We wobbled towards the lodge and saw Diane talking to Greg.

She looked up. "Roxanne! So you made it down."

"With Keri's help. She talked me down," Roxanne said.

Diane's eyes opened wide. She looked at me, to Roxanne, then back to me. "Grizzly Bowl? Keri? You went up there?"

I nodded.

And there it was. A look of awe in Diane's eyes, the look of admiration that I had been longing for, praying for so long. She laughed nervously. "Kinda steep, wasn't it?"

"Yeah, kinda steep," I said. "And I'm kinda worn out." I turned to Roxanne. "We'd better go sit down."

Steve and Ron came in a few minutes later. "Keri, we've been looking all over for you. We were so worried. Where were you?"

I raised my head and sighed. "Would you believe Grizzly Bowl?"

They both laughed. "Oh, sure, tell us about it."

"I will. When I get up the energy—and the nerve. Maybe in a week or two."

Steve's eyes widened. "Grizzly Bowl? Really?"

I nodded.

Then, with intense pride and gentleness, he murmured, "Keri . . ."

I slept on the bus all the way home. That sleep was one of the deepest, most refreshing I'd ever had. I slept as though drugged, and awoke feeling like a different person, still aching, still tired, but refreshed deep within.

When the bus pulled into the school yard, I saw Mom, Dad, and Colleen waiting beside our car, chatting with the Spaldings.

"How did you get along, Keri?" Dad asked.

"Well, I made it down some pretty tough slopes, and it turned out to be not too bad after all."

When Colleen and I crawled into the back seat, she nudged me and said, "I bet it was quite a day."

It had started to snow, big, soft, wet flakes. In the dark coziness of the back seat I leaned against Colleen, listening to the hypnotizing rhythm of the wiper blades, and awoke, startled to find that we were already home.

As I climbed out of the car, Mom put her arm around me and said gently, "You must be ready for bed, eh?"

Then the crazy idea came to me. I had to do it tonight. Yes, while all this was still fresh and nothing else could possibly seem as scary.

"You guys go ahead. I'm just going to stay out here for a little while. I need some time to be alone. I'll come in soon. Please."

They started to argue with me, but then Dad shrugged his shoulders. "If you feel like tramping around out here in the snow and dark, I guess you have a right to do it. But don't stay out too long. You've really had enough for one day, Skalawag." He ruffled my hair and gave me a hug. "Better put your toque on."

I stood alone in the silence, watching thousands of huge snowflakes drifting and spinning against the yard light, then turned my weary legs and walked towards the dark barn. "Sandy, this is for you."

When I came back into the house, blinking at the brightness of the lights, shaking off the snow, Colleen looked at my tired shining eyes and she grinned, the broadest, deepest grin I'd ever seen in my life. And I knew that she knew.

She didn't say anything about it, though, until I got into bed, and pulled the puffy quilt up around my neck. Then she sat on my bed. "You did it, tonight, didn't you? You cantered on Fancy, didn't you?"

There was no need to answer. Tears ran across my face, and I didn't even try to wipe them away.

"Weren't you scared?"

"Yeah, I sure was."

About the Author

Irene Morck was born in Saint John, New Brunswick, but has spent much of her life on the prairies, apart from two years in Barbados and then ten years in Jamaica where she did research in biochemistry at the University of the West Indies and taught at a boys' school.

Since 1979 Irene has lived on a farm near Spruce View, Alberta, with her husband, Mogens Nielsen. Together they raise cattle, hay, and grain and take part in a variety of leisure-time activities including photography, trail riding, canoeing, cross-country skiing, and travelling. They have no children but lots of animals – a herd of cattle, eight horses, two baby mules, five cats, two dogs, and two budgies.

Irene has been a freelance writer for many years and has had her work published in magazines across Canada and the USA. *A Question of Courage* is her first novel.